EDGEDANCER

Also by Brandon Sanderson from Gollancz:

EDGEDANCER

BRANDON SANDERSON

GOLLANCZ
LONDON

This edition first published in Great Britain in 2018 by Gollancz.

First published in Great Britain in 2016 by Gollancz
an imprint of the Orion Publishing Group Ltd
Carmelite House, 50 Victoria Embankment
London EC4Y 0DZ

An Hachette UK Company

1 3 5 7 9 10 8 6 4 2

A CIP catalogue record for this book is
available from the British Library.

ISBN 978 1 473 22503 9

Printed and bound in Great Britain
by Clays Ltd, Elcograf S.p.A.

www.brandonsanderson.com
www.gollancz.co.uk

EDGEDANCER

This story takes place after and contains spoilers for *Words of Radiance*.

PROLOGUE

Lift had never robbed a palace before. Seemed like a dangerous thing to try. Not because she might get caught, but because once you robbed a starvin' palace, where did you go next?

She climbed up onto the outer wall and looked in at the grounds. Everything inside—trees, rocks, buildings—reflected the starlight in an odd way. A bulbous-looking building stuck up in the middle of it all, like a bubble on a pond. In fact, most of the buildings were that same round shape, often with small protrusions sprouting out of the top. There wasn't a straight line in the whole starvin' place. Just lots and lots of curves.

Lift's companions climbed up to peek over the top of the wall. A scuffling, scrambling, rowdy mess they were. Six men, supposedly master thieves. They couldn't even climb a wall properly.

"The Bronze Palace itself," Huqin breathed.

"Bronze? Is that what everythin' is made of?" Lift asked, sitting on the wall with one leg over the side. "Looks like a bunch of breasts."

The men looked at her, aghast. They were all Azish, with dark skin and hair. She was Reshi, from the islands up north. Her mother had told her that, though Lift had never seen the place.

"What?" Huqin demanded.

"Breasts," Lift said, pointing. "See, like a lady layin' on her back. Those points on the tops are nipples. Bloke who built this place musta been single for a *looong* time."

Huqin turned to one of his companions. Using their ropes, they scuttled back down the outside of the wall to hold a whispered conference.

"Grounds at this end look empty, as my informant indicated would be the case," Huqin said. He was in charge of the lot of them. Had a nose like someone had taken hold of it when he was a kid and pulled real, *real* hard. Lift was surprised he didn't smack people in the face with it when he turned.

"Everyone's focused on choosing the new Prime Aqasix," said Maxin. "We could really do this. Rob the Bronze Palace itself, and right under the nose of the vizierate."

"Is it . . . um . . . safe?" asked Huqin's nephew. He was

in his teens, and puberty hadn't been kind to him. Not with that face, that voice, and those spindly legs.

"Hush," Huqin snapped.

"No," Tigzikk said, "the boy is right to express caution. This will be very dangerous."

Tigzikk was considered the learned one in the group on account of his being able to cuss in three languages. Downright scholarly, that was. He wore fancy clothing, while most of the others wore black. "There will be chaos," Tigzikk continued, "because so many people move through the palace tonight, but there will also be danger. Many, many bodyguards and a likelihood of suspicion on all sides."

Tigzikk was an aging fellow, and was the only one of the group Lift knew well. She couldn't say his name. That "quq" sound on the end of his name sounded like choking when someone pronounced it correctly. She just called him Tig instead.

"Tigzikk," Huqin said. Yup. Choking. "You were the one who suggested this. Don't tell me you're getting cold now."

"I'm not backing down. I'm pleading caution."

Lift leaned down over the wall toward them. "Less arguing," she said. "Let's move. I'm hungry."

Huqin looked up. "*Why* did we bring her along?"

"She'll be useful," Tigzikk said. "You'll see."

"She's just a child!"

"She's a youth. She's at least twelve."

"I *ain't* twelve," Lift snapped, looming over them.

They turned up toward her.

"I ain't," she said. "Twelve's an unlucky number." She held up her hands. "I'm only this many."

". . . Ten?" Tigzikk asked.

"Is that how many that is? Sure, then. Ten." She lowered her hands. "If I can't count it on my fingers, it's unlucky." And she'd been that many for three years now. So there.

"Seems like there are a lot of unlucky ages," Huqin said, sounding amused.

"Sure are," she agreed. She scanned the grounds again, then glanced back the way they had come, into the city.

A man walked down one of the streets leading to the palace. His dark clothing blended into the gloom, but his silver buttons glinted each time he passed a streetlight.

Storms, she thought, a chill running up her spine. *I didn't lose him after all.*

She looked down at the men. "Are you coming with me or not? 'Cuz I'm *leaving*." She slipped over the top and dropped into the palace yards. Lift squatted there, feeling the cold ground. Yup, it was metal. Everything was bronze. Rich people, she decided, loved to stick with a theme.

As the boys finally stopped arguing and started climbing, a thin, twisting trail of vines grew out of the darkness and approached Lift. It looked like a little stream of spilled water picking its way across the floor. Here and there, bits of clear crystal peeked out of the vines, like sections of quartz in otherwise dark stone. Those weren't sharp, but smooth like polished glass, and didn't glow with Stormlight.

The vines grew super-fast, curling about one another in a tangle that formed a face.

"Mistress," the face said. "Is this *wise*?"

" 'Ello, Voidbringer," Lift said, scanning the grounds.

"I am *not* a Voidbringer!" he said. "And you know it. Just . . . just stop saying that!"

Lift grinned. "You're my pet Voidbringer, and no lies are going to change that. I got you captured. No stealing souls, now. We ain't here for souls. Just a little thievery, the type what never hurt nobody."

The vine face—he called himself Wyndle—sighed. Lift scuttled across the bronze ground over to a tree that was, of course, also made of bronze. Huqin had chosen the darkest part of night, between moons, for them to slip in—but the starlight was enough to see by on a cloudless night like this.

Wyndle grew up to her, leaving a small trail of vines that people didn't seem to be able to see. The vines hardened after a few moments of sitting, as if briefly becoming solid crystal, then they crumbled to dust. People spotted that on occasion, though they certainly couldn't see Wyndle himself.

"I'm a spren," Wyndle said to her. "Part of a proud and noble—"

"Hush," Lift said, peeking out from behind the bronze tree. An open-topped carriage passed on the drive beyond, carrying some important Azish folk. You could tell by the coats. Big, drooping coats with really wide sleeves and patterns that argued with each other. They all looked like kids who had snuck into their parents' wardrobe. The hats were nifty, though.

The thieves followed behind her, moving with reasonable stealth. They really weren't *that* bad. Even if they didn't know how to climb a wall properly.

They gathered around her, and Tigzikk stood up, straightening his coat—which was an imitation of one of those worn by the rich scribe types who worked in the government. Here in Azir, working for the government was real important. Everyone else was said to be "discrete," whatever that meant.

"Ready?" Tigzikk said to Maxin, who was the other one of the thieves dressed in fine clothing.

Maxin nodded, and the two of them moved off to the right, heading toward the palace's sculpture garden. The important people would supposedly be shuffling around in there, speculating about who should be the next Prime.

Dangerous job, that. The last two had gotten their heads chopped off by some bloke in white with a Shardblade. The most recent Prime hadn't lasted two starvin' days!

With Tigzikk and Maxin gone, Lift only had four others to worry about. Huqin, his nephew, and two slender brothers who didn't talk much and kept reaching under their coats for knives. Lift didn't like their type. Thieving shouldn't leave bodies. Leaving bodies was easy. There was no *challenge* to it if you could just kill anyone who spotted you.

"You *can* get us in," Huqin said to Lift. "Right?"

Lift pointedly rolled her eyes. Then she scuttled across the bronze grounds toward the main palace structure.

Really does look like a breast...

Wyndle curled along the ground beside her, his vine trail sprouting tiny bits of clear crystal here and there. He was as sinuous and speedy as a moving eel, only he *grew* rather than actually moving. Voidbringers were a strange lot.

"You realize that *I* didn't choose you," he said, a face appearing in the vines as they moved. His speaking left a strange effect, the trail behind him clotted with a sequence of frozen faces. The mouth seemed to move because it was growing so quickly beside her. "*I* wanted to pick a distinguished Iriali matron. A grandmother, an accomplished gardener. But no, the Ring said we should choose you. 'She has visited the Old Magic,' they said. 'Our mother has blessed her,' they said. 'She will be young, and we can mold her,' they said. Well, *they* don't have to put up with—"

"Shut it, Voidbringer," Lift hissed, drawing up beside the wall of the palace. "Or I'll bathe in blessed water and go listen to the priests. Maybe get an exorcism."

Lift edged sideways until she could look around the curve of the wall to spot the guard patrol: men in patterned vests and caps, with long halberds. She looked up the side of the wall. It bulged out just above her, like a rockbud, before tapering up further. It was of smooth bronze, with no handholds.

She waited until the guards had walked farther away. "All right," she whispered to Wyndle. "You gotta do what I say."

"I do *not.*"

"Sure you do. I captured you, just like in the stories."

"I came to *you*," Wyndle said. "Your powers come from me! Do you even *listen* to—"

"Up the wall," Lift said, pointing.

Wyndle sighed, but obeyed, creeping up the wall in a wide, looping pattern. Lift hopped up, grabbing the small handholds made by the vine, which stuck to the surface by virtue of thousands of branching stems with sticky discs on them. Wyndle wove ahead of her, making a ladder of sorts.

It wasn't easy. It was starvin' difficult, with that bulge, and Wyndle's handholds weren't very big. But she did it, climbing all the way to the near-top of the building's dome, where windows peeked out at the grounds.

She glanced toward the city. No sign of the man in the black uniform. Maybe she'd lost him.

She turned back to examine the window. Its nice wooden frame held very thick glass, even though it pointed east. It was unfair how well Azimir was protected from highstorms. They should have to live with the wind, like normal folk.

"We need to Voidbring that," she said, pointing at the window.

"Have you realized," Wyndle said, "that while you *claim* to be a master thief, *I* do all of the work in this relationship?"

"You do all the complainin' too," she said. "How do we get through this?"

"You have the seeds?"

She nodded, fishing in her pocket. Then in the other one. Then in her back pocket. Ah, there they were. She pulled out a handful of seeds.

"I can't affect the Physical Realm except in minor ways," Wyndle said. "This means that you will need to use Investiture to—"

Lift yawned.

"Use Investiture to—"

She yawned *wider*. Starvin' Voidbringers never could catch a hint.

Wyndle sighed. "Spread the seeds on the frame."

She did so, throwing the handful of seeds at the window.

"Your bond to me grants two primary classes of ability," Wyndle said. "The first, manipulation of friction, you've already—don't yawn at me!—discovered. We have been using that well for many weeks now, and it is time for you to learn the second, the power of Growth. You aren't ready for what was once known as Regrowth, the healing of—"

Lift pressed her hand against the seeds, then summoned her awesomeness.

She wasn't sure how she did it. She just *did*. It had started right around when Wyndle had first appeared.

He hadn't talked then. She kind of missed those days.

Her hand glowed faintly with white light, like vapor coming off the skin. The seeds that saw the light started to grow. Fast. Vines burst from the seeds and wormed into the cracks between the window and its frame.

The vines grew at her will, making constricted, straining sounds. The glass cracked, then the window frame *popped* open.

Lift grinned.

"Well done," Wyndle said. "We'll make an Edgedancer out of you yet."

Her stomach grumbled. When had she last eaten? She'd used a lot of her awesomeness practicing earlier. She probably should have stolen something to eat. She wasn't quite so awesome when she was hungry.

She slipped inside the window. Having a Voidbringer was useful, though she wasn't *completely* sure her powers came from him. That seemed the sorta thing a Voidbringer would lie about. She *had* captured him, fair and square. She'd used words. A Voidbringer had no body, not really. To catch something like that, you had to use words. Everybody knew it. Just like curses made evil things come find you.

She had to get out a sphere—a diamond mark, her lucky one—to see properly in here. The small bedroom was decorated after the Azish way with lots of intricate patterns on the rugs and the fabric on the walls, mostly gold and red here. Those patterns were everything to the Azish. They were like words.

She looked out the window. Surely she'd escaped Darkness, the man in the black and silver with the pale crescent birthmark on his cheek. The man with the dead, lifeless stare. Surely he hadn't followed her all the way from Marabethia. That was half a continent away! Well, a quarter one, at the least.

Convinced, she uncoiled the rope that she wore wrapped around her waist and over her shoulders. She tied it to the door of a built-in closet, then fed it out the window. It tightened as the men started climbing. Nearby, Wyndle grew up around one of the bedposts, coiled like a skyeel.

She heard whispered voices below. "Did you *see* that? She climbed right up it. Not a handhold in sight. How . . . ?"

"Hush." That was Huqin.

Lift began poking through cabinets and drawers as the boys clambered in the window one at a time. Once inside, the thieves pulled up the rope and shut the window as best they could. Huqin studied the vines she'd grown from seeds on the frame.

Lift stuck her head in the bottom of a wardrobe, groping around. "Ain't nothing in this room but moldy shoes."

"You," Huqin said to her, "and my nephew will hold this room. The three of us will search the bedrooms nearby. We will be back shortly."

"You'll probably have a whole *sack* of moldy shoes . . ." Lift said, pulling out of the wardrobe.

"Ignorant child," Huqin said, pointing at the wardrobe. One of his men grabbed the shoes and outfits inside, stuffing them in a sack. "This clothing will sell for bundles. It's exactly what we're looking for."

"What about real riches?" Lift said. "Spheres, jewelry, art . . ." She had little interest in those things herself, but she'd figured it was what Huqin was after.

"That will all be *far* too well guarded," Huqin said as his two associates made quick work of the room's clothing. "The difference between a successful thief and a dead thief is knowing when to escape with your takings. This haul will let us live in luxury for a year or two. That is enough."

One of the brothers peeked out the door into the hallway. He nodded, and the three of them slipped out. "Listen for the warning," Huqin said to his nephew, then eased the door almost closed behind him.

Tigzikk and his accomplice below would listen for any kind of alarm. If anything seemed to be amiss, they'd slip off and blow their whistles. Huqin's nephew crouched by the window to listen, obviously taking his duty very seriously. He looked to be about sixteen. Unlucky age, that.

"How did you climb the wall like that?" the youth asked.

"Gumption," Lift said. "And spit."

He frowned at her.

"I gots magic spit."

He seemed to believe her. Idiot.

"Is it strange for you here?" he asked. "Away from your people?"

She stood out. Straight black hair—she wore it down to her waist—tan skin, rounded features. Everyone would immediately mark her as Reshi.

"Don't know," Lift said, strolling to the door. "Ain't never been around my people."

"You're not from the islands?"

"Nope. Grew up in Rall Elorim."

"The . . . City of Shadows?"

"Yup."

"Is it—"

"Yup. Just like they say."

She peeked through the door. Huqin and the others were well out of the way. The hallway was bronze— walls and everything—but a red and blue rug, with lots of little vine patterns, ran down the center. Paintings hung on the walls.

She pulled the door all the way open and stepped out.

"Lift!" The nephew scrambled to the door. "They told us to wait here!"

"And?"

"And we should *wait here*! We don't want to get Uncle Huqin in trouble!"

"What's the point of sneaking into a palace if not to

get into trouble?" She shook her head. Odd men, these. "This should be an interesting place, what with all of the rich folk hanging around." There ought to be some *really* good food in here.

She padded out into the hallway, and Wyndle grew along the floor beside her. Interestingly, the nephew followed. She'd expected him to stay in the room.

"We shouldn't be doing this," he said as they passed a door that was open a crack, shuffles sounding from inside. Huqin and his men, robbing the place silly.

"Then stay," Lift whispered, reaching a large stairwell. Servants whisked back and forth below, even a few parshmen, but she didn't catch sight of anyone in one of those coats. "Where are the important folk?"

"Reading forms," the nephew said from beside her.

"Forms?"

"Sure," he said. "With the Prime dead, the viziers, scribes, and arbiters were all given a chance to fill out the proper paperwork to apply to take his place."

"You *apply* to be emperor?" Lift said.

"Sure," he said. "Lots of paperwork involved in that. And an essay. Your essay has to be *really* good to get this job."

"Storms. You people are crazy."

"Other nations do it better? With bloody succession wars? This way, everyone has a chance. Even the lowest of clerks can submit the paperwork. You can even be *discrete* and end up on the throne, if you are convincing enough. It happened once."

"Crazy."

"Says the girl who talks to herself."

Lift looked at him sharply.

"Don't pretend you don't," he said. "I've seen you doing it. Talking to the air, as if somebody were there."

"What's your name?" she asked.

"Gawx."

"Wow. Well then, Gaw. I don't talk to myself because I'm crazy."

"No?"

"I do it because I'm *awesome*." She started down the steps, waited for a gap between passing servants, then made for a closet across the way. Gawx cursed, then followed.

Lift was tempted to use her awesomeness to slide across the floor quickly, but she didn't need that yet. Besides, Wyndle kept complaining that she used the awesomeness too often. That she was at risk of malnutrition, whatever that meant.

She slipped up to the closet, using just her normal everyday sneakin' skills, and moved inside. Gawx scrambled into the closet with her just before she pulled it shut. Dinnerware on a serving cart clinked behind them, and they could barely crowd into the space. Gawx moved, causing more clinks, and she elbowed him. He stilled as two parshmen passed, bearing large wine barrels.

"You should go back upstairs," Lift whispered to him. "This could be dangerous."

"Oh, sneaking into the storming *royal palace* is dangerous? Thanks. I hadn't realized."

"I mean it," Lift said, peeking out of the closet. "Go back up, leave when Huqin returns. He'll abandon me in a heartbeat. Probably will you, too."

Besides, she didn't want to be awesome with Gawx around. That started questions. And rumors. She hated both. For once, she'd like to be able to stay someplace for a while without being forced to run off.

"No," Gawx said softly. "If you're going to steal something good, I want a piece of it. Then maybe Huqin will stop making me stay behind, giving me the easy jobs."

Huh. So he had some spunk to him.

A servant passed carrying a large, plate-filled tray. The food smells wafting from it made Lift's stomach growl. Rich-person food. So *delicious*.

Lift watched the woman go, then broke out of the closet, following after. This was going to get difficult with Gawx in tow. He'd been trained well enough by his uncle, but moving unseen through a populated building wasn't easy.

The serving woman pulled open a door that was

hidden in the wall. Servants' hallways. Lift caught it as it closed, waited a few heartbeats, then eased it open and slipped through. The narrow hallway was poorly lit and smelled of the food that had just passed.

Gawx entered behind Lift, then silently pulled the door closed. The serving woman disappeared around a corner ahead—there were probably lots of hallways like this in the palace. Behind Lift, Wyndle grew around the doorframe, a dark green, funguslike creep of vines that covered the door, then the wall beside her.

He formed a face in the vines and spots of crystal, then shook his head.

"Too narrow?" Lift asked.

He nodded.

"It's dark in here. Hard to see us."

"Vibrations on the floor, mistress. Someone coming this direction."

She looked longingly after the servant with the food, then shoved past Gawx and pushed open the door, entering the main hallways again.

Gawx cursed. "Do you even know what you're doing?"

"No," she said, then scuttled around a corner into a large hallway lined with alternating green and yellow gemstone lamps. Unfortunately, a servant in a stiff, black and white uniform was coming right at her.

Gawx let out a "meep" of worry, ducking back around the corner. Lift stood up straight, clasped her hands behind her back, and strolled forward.

She passed the man. His uniform marked him as someone important, for a servant.

"You, there!" the man snapped. "What is this?"

"Mistress wants some cake," Lift said, jutting out her chin.

"Oh, for Yaezir's sake. Food is served in the gardens! There is cake *there*!"

"Wrong type," Lift said. "Mistress wants berry cake."

The man threw his hands into the air. "Kitchens are back the other way," he said. "Try and persuade the cook, though she'll probably chop your hands off before she takes another special request. Storming country scribes! Special dietary needs are supposed to be sent ahead of time, with the proper forms!" He stalked off, leaving Lift with hands behind her back, watching him.

Gawk slunk around the corner. "I thought we were dead for sure."

"Don't be stupid," Lift said, hurrying down the hallway. "This ain't the dangerous part yet."

At the other end, this hallway intersected another one—with the same wide rug down the center, bronze walls, and glowing metal lamps. Across the way was a door with no light shining under it. Lift checked in both directions, then dashed to the door, cracked it, peeked in, then waved for Gawx to join her inside.

"We should go right down that hallway outside," Gawx whispered as she shut the door all but a crack. "Down that way, we'll find the vizier quarters. They're probably empty, because everyone will be in the Prime's wing deliberating."

"You know the palace layout?" she asked, crouching in near darkness beside the door. They were in a small sitting room of some sort, with a couple of shadowed chairs and a small table.

"Yeah," Gawx said. "I memorized the palace maps before we came. You didn't?"

She shrugged.

"I've been in here once before," Gawx said. "I watched the Prime sleeping."

"You *what*?"

"He's public," Gawx said, "belongs to everyone. You can enter a lottery to come look at him sleeping. They rotate people through every hour."

"What? On a special day or something?"

"No, every day. You can watch him eat too, or watch him perform his daily rituals. If he loses a hair or cuts off a nail, you might be able to keep it as a relic."

"Sounds creepy."

"A little."

"Which way to his rooms?" Lift asked.

"That way," Gawx said, pointing left down the hallway outside—the opposite direction from the vizier chambers. "You don't want to go there, Lift. That's where the viziers and everyone important will be reviewing applications. In the Prime's presence."

"But he's dead."

"The new Prime."

"He ain't been chosen yet!"

"Well, it's kind of strange," Gawx said. By the dim light of the cracked door, she could see him blushing, as if he knew how starvin' odd this all was. "There's never *not* a Prime. We just don't know who he is yet. I mean, he's alive, and he's already Prime—right now. We're just catching up. So, those are his quarters, and the scions and viziers want to be in his presence while they decide who he is. Even if the person they decide upon isn't in the room."

"That makes no sense."

"Of course it makes sense," Gawx said. "It's government. This is all *very* well detailed in the codes and . . ." He trailed off as Lift yawned. Azish could be *real* boring. At least he could take a hint, though.

"Anyway," Gawx continued, "everyone outside in the gardens is hoping to be called in for a personal interview. It might not come to that, though. The scions can't be Prime, as they're too busy visiting and blessing villages around the kingdom—but a vizier can, and they tend to have the best applications. Usually, one of their number is chosen."

"The Prime's quarters," Lift said. "That's the direction the food went."

"What is it with you and food?"

"I'm going to eat their dinner," she said, soft but intense.

Gawx blinked, startled. "You're . . . *what*?"

"I'm gonna eat their food," she said. "Rich folk have the best food."

"But . . . there might be spheres in the vizier quarters. . . ."

"Eh," she said. "I'd just spend 'em on food."

Stealing regular stuff was no fun. She wanted a *real* challenge. Over the last two years, she'd picked the most difficult places to enter. Then she'd snuck in.

And eaten their dinners.

"Come on," she said, moving out of the doorway, then turned left toward the Prime's chambers.

"You really *are* crazy," Gawx whispered.

"Nah. Just bored."

He looked the other way. "I'm going for the vizier quarters."

"Suit yourself," she said. "I'd go back upstairs instead, if I were you. You aren't practiced enough for this kind of thing. You leave me, you're probably going to get into trouble."

He fidgeted, then slipped off in the direction of the vizier quarters. Lift rolled her eyes.

"Why did you even come with them?" Wyndle asked, creeping out of the room. "Why not just sneak in on your own?"

"Tigzikk found out about this whole election thing," she said. "He told me tonight was a good night for sneaking. I owed it to him. Besides, I wanted to be here in case he got into trouble. I might need to help."

"Why bother?"

Why indeed? "Someone has to care," she said, starting down the hallway. "Too few people care, these days."

"You say this while coming in to *rob* people."

"Sure. Ain't gonna hurt them."

"You have an odd sense of morality, mistress."

"Don't be stupid," she said. "Every sense of morality is odd."

"I suppose."

"Particularly to a Voidbringer."

"I'm not—"

She grinned and hurried her pace toward the Prime's quarters. She knew she'd found those when she glanced down a side hallway and spotted guards at the end. Yup. That door was so nice, it *had* to belong to an emperor. Only super-rich folk built fancy doors. You needed money coming out your ears before you spent it on a *door*.

Guards were a problem. Lift knelt down, peeking around the corner. The hallway leading to the emperor's rooms was narrow, like an alleyway. Smart. Hard to sneak down something like that. And those two guards, they weren't the bored type. They were the "we gotta stand here and look real angry" type. They stood so straight, you'd have thought someone had shoved brooms up their backsides.

She glanced upward. The hallway was tall; rich folk liked tall stuff. If they'd been poor, they'd have built another floor up there for their aunts and cousins to live in. Rich people wasted space instead. Proved they had so much money, they could waste it.

Seemed perfectly rational to steal from them.

"There," Lift whispered, pointing to a small ornamented ledge that ran along the wall up above. It wouldn't be wide enough to walk on, unless you were Lift. Which, fortunately, she was. It was dim up there too. The chandeliers were the dangly kind, and they hung low, with mirrors reflecting their spherelight downward.

"Up we go," she said.

Wyndle sighed.

"You gotta do what I say or I'll prune you."

"You'll . . . prune me."

"Sure." That sounded threatening, right?

Wyndle grew up the wall, giving her handholds.

Already, the vines he'd trailed through the hallway behind them were vanishing, becoming crystal and disintegrating into dust.

"Why don't they notice you?" Lift whispered. She'd never asked him, despite their months together. "Is it 'cuz only the pure in heart can see you?"

"You're not serious."

"Sure. That'd fit into legends and stories and stuff."

"Oh, the theory itself isn't ridiculous," Wyndle said, speaking out of a bit of vine near her, the various cords of green moving like lips. "Merely the idea that *you* consider yourself to be pure in heart."

"I'm pure," Lift whispered, grunting as she climbed. "I'm a child and stuff. I'm so storming pure I practically belch rainbows."

Wyndle sighed again—he liked to do that—as they reached the ledge. Wyndle grew along the side of it, making it slightly wider, and Lift stepped onto it. She balanced carefully, then nodded to Wyndle. He grew further along the ledge, then doubled back and grew up the wall to a point above her head. From there, he grew horizontally to give her a handhold. With the extra inch of vine on the ledge and the hand-hold above, she managed to sidle along, stomach to the wall. She took a deep breath, then turned the corner into the hallway with the guards.

She moved along it slowly, Wyndle wrapping back

and forth, enhancing both footing and handholds for her. The guards didn't cry out. She was *doing* it.

"They can't see me," Wyndle said, growing up beside her to create another line of handholds, "because I exist mostly in the Cognitive Realm, even though I've moved my consciousness to this Realm. I can make myself visible to anyone, should I desire, though it's not easy for me. Other spren are more skilled at it, while some have the opposite trouble. Of course, no matter *how* I manifest, nobody can touch me, as I barely have any substance in this Realm."

"Nobody but me," Lift whispered, inching down the hallway.

"You shouldn't be able to either," he said, sounding troubled. "What did you ask for, when you visited my mother?"

Lift didn't have to answer that, not to a storming Voidbringer. She eventually reached the end of the hallway. Beneath her was the door. Unfortunately, that was exactly where the guards stood.

"This does not seem very well thought out, mistress," Wyndle noted. "Had you considered *what* you were going to do once you got here?"

She nodded.

"Well?"

"Wait," she whispered.

They did, Lift with her front pressed to the wall, her

heels hanging out above a fifteen-foot drop onto the guards. She didn't want to fall. She was pretty sure she was awesome enough to survive it, but if they saw her, that would end the game. She'd have to run, and she'd *never* get any dinner.

Fortunately, she'd guessed right, unfortunately. A guard appeared at the other end of the hallway, looking out of breath and not a little annoyed. The other two guards jogged over to him. He turned, pointing the other way.

That was her chance. Wyndle grew a vine downward, and Lift grabbed it. She could feel the crystals jutting out between the tendrils, but they were smooth and faceted—not angular and sharp. She dropped, vine smooth between her fingers, pulling herself to a stop just before the floor.

She only had a few seconds.

". . . caught a thief trying to ransack the vizier quarters," said the newer guard. "Might be more. Keep watch. By Yaezir himself! I can't believe they'd dare. Tonight of all nights!"

Lift cracked open the door to the emperor's rooms and peeked in. Big room. Men and women at a table. Nobody looking her direction. She slipped through the door.

Then became awesome.

She ducked down, kicked herself forward, and for

a moment, the floor—the carpet, the wood beneath—had no purchase on her. She glided as if on ice, making no noise as she slid across the ten-foot gap. Nothing could hold her when she got Slick like this. Fingers would slip off her, and she could glide forever. She didn't think she'd ever stop unless she turned off the awesomeness. She'd slide all the way to the storming ocean itself.

Tonight, she stopped herself under the table, using her fingers—which weren't Slick—then removed the Slickness from her legs. Her stomach growled in complaint. She needed food. Real fast, or no more awesomeness for her.

"Somehow, you are partly in the Cognitive Realm," Wyndle said, coiling beside her and raising a twisting mesh of vines that could make a face. "It is the only answer I can find to why you can touch spren. And you can metabolize food *directly* into Stormlight."

She shrugged. He was always saying words like those. Trying to confuse her, starvin' Voidbringer. Well, she wouldn't talk back to him, not now. The men and women standing around the table might hear her, even if they couldn't hear Wyndle.

That food was in here somewhere. She could smell it.

"But *why*?" Wyndle said. "Why did She give you this incredible talent? Why a child? There are soldiers, grand kings, incredible scholars among humankind. Instead she chose you."

Food, food, food. Smelled *great*. Lift crawled along under the long table. The men and women up above were talking in very concerned voices.

"Your application was *clearly* the best, Dalksi."

"What! I misspelled three words in the first paragraph alone!"

"I didn't notice."

"You didn't... Of course you noticed! But this is pointless, because *Axikk's* essay was obviously superior to mine."

"Don't bring me into this again. We disqualified me. I'm not fit to be Prime. I have a bad back."

"Ashno of Sages had a bad back. He was one of the greatest Emuli Primes."

"Bah! My essay was utter rubbish, and you know it."

Wyndle moved along beside Lift. "Mother has given up on your kind. I can feel it. She doesn't care any longer. Now that He's gone ..."

"This arguing does not befit us," said a commanding female voice. "We should take our vote. People are waiting."

"Let it go to one of those fools in the gardens."

"Their essays were *dreadful*. Just look at what Pandri wrote across the top of hers."

"My . . . I . . . I don't know what half of that even means, but it *does* seem insulting."

This finally caught Lift's attention. She looked up toward the table above. Good cusses? *Come on,* she thought. *Read a few of those.*

"We'll have to pick one of them," the other voice—she sounded very in charge—said. "Kadasixes and Stars, this is a puzzle. What do we do when *nobody* wants to be Prime?"

Nobody wanted to be Prime? Had the entire country suddenly grown some sense? Lift continued on. Being rich seemed fun and all, but being in charge of that many people? Pure misery, that would be.

"Perhaps we should pick the *worst* application," one of the voices said. "In this situation, that would indicate the cleverest applicant."

"Six different monarchs killed . . ." one of the voices said, a new one. "In a mere two months. Highprinces slaughtered throughout the East. Religious leaders. And then, two Primes murdered in a matter of a single week. Storms . . . I almost think it's another Desolation come upon us."

"A Desolation in the form of a single man. Yaezir help the one we choose. It is a death sentence."

"We have stalled too long as it is. These weeks of waiting with no Prime have been harmful to Azir. Let's just pick the worst application. From this stack."

"What if we pick someone who is legitimately terrible? Is it not our *duty* to care for the kingdom, regardless of the risk to the one we choose?"

"But in picking the best from among us, we doom our brightest, our best, to die by the sword . . . Yaezir help us. Scion Ethid, a prayer for guidance would be appreciated. We need Yaezir himself to show us his will. Perhaps if we choose the right person, he or she will be protected by his hand."

Lift reached the end of the table and looked out at a banquet that had been set onto a smaller table at the other side of the room. This place was *very* Azish. Curls of embroidery everywhere. Carpets so fine, they probably drove some poor woman blind weaving them. Dark colors and dim lights. Paintings on the walls.

Huh, Lift thought, *someone scratched a face off of that one.* Who'd ruin a painting like that, and such a fine one, the Heralds all in a row?

Well, nobody seemed to be touching that feast. Her stomach growled, but she waited for a distraction.

It came soon after. The door opened. Likely the guards coming to report about the thief they'd found. Poor Gawx. She'd have to go break him out later.

Right now, it was time for food. Lift shoved herself forward on her knees and used her awesomeness to Slick her legs. She slid across the floor and grabbed the corner leg of the food table. Her momentum smoothly pivoted her around and behind it. She crouched down, the tablecloth neatly hiding her from the people at the room's center, and unSlicked her legs.

Perfect. She reached up a hand and plucked a dinner roll off the table. She took a bite, then hesitated.

Why had everyone grown quiet? She risked a glance over the tabletop.

He had arrived.

The tall Azish man with the white mark on his cheek, like a crescent. Black uniform with a double row of silver buttons down the coat's front, a stiff silver collar poking up from a shirt underneath. His thick gloves had collars of their own that extended halfway back around his forearms.

Dead eyes. This was Darkness himself.

Oh no.

"What is the meaning of this!" demanded one of the viziers, a woman in one of their large coats with the too-big sleeves. Her cap was of a different pattern, and it clashed quite spectacularly with the coat.

"I am here," Darkness said, "for a thief."

"Do you realize where you are? How *dare* you interrupt—"

"I have," Darkness said, "the proper forms." He spoke completely without emotion. No annoyance at being challenged, no arrogance or pomposity. Nothing at all. One of his minions entered behind him, a man in a black and silver uniform, less ornamented. He proffered a neat stack of papers to his master.

"Forms are all well and good," the vizier said. "But this is *not* the time, constable, for—"

Lift bolted.

Her instincts finally battered down her surprise and she ran, leaping over a couch on her way to the room's back door. Wyndle moved beside her in a streak.

She tore a hunk off the roll with her teeth; she was going to need the food. Beyond that door would be a bedroom, and a bedroom would have a window. She slammed open the door, dashing through.

Something swung from the shadows on the other side.

A cudgel took her in the chest. Ribs cracked. Lift gasped, dropping face-first to the floor.

Another of Darkness's minions stepped from the shadows inside the bedroom.

"Even the chaotic," Darkness said, "can be predictable with proper study." His feet thumped across the floor behind her.

Lift gritted her teeth, curled up on the floor. *Didn't get enough to eat* . . . So hungry.

The few bites she'd taken earlier worked within her. She felt the familiar feeling, like a storm in her veins.

Liquid awesomeness. The pain faded from her chest as she healed.

Wyndle ran around her in a circle, a little lasso of vines sprouting leaves on the floor, looping her again and again. Darkness stepped up close.

Go! She leaped to her hands and knees. He seized her by the shoulder, but she could escape that. She summoned her awesomeness.

Darkness thrust something toward her.

The little animal was like a cremling, but with *wings*. Bound wings, tied-up legs. It had a strange little face, not crabbish like a cremling. More like a tiny axehound, with a snout, mouth, and eyes.

It seemed sickly, and its shimmering eyes were pained. How could she tell that?

The creature sucked the awesomeness from Lift. She actually *saw* it go, a glistening whiteness that streamed from her to the little animal. It opened its mouth, drinking it in.

Suddenly, Lift felt very tired and very, *very* hungry.

Darkness handed the animal to one of his minions, who made it vanish into a black sack he then tucked in his pocket. Lift was certain that the viziers—standing in an outraged cluster at the table—hadn't seen any of this, not with Darkness's back to them and the two minions crowding around.

"Keep all spheres from her," Darkness said. "She must not be allowed to Invest."

Lift felt terror, panicked in a way she hadn't known for years, ever since her days in Rall Elorim. She struggled, thrashing, biting at the hand that held her. Darkness didn't even grunt. He hauled her to her feet, and another minion took her by the arms, wrenching them backward until she gasped at the pain.

No. She'd freed herself! She couldn't be taken like this. Wyndle continued to spin around her on the ground, distressed. He was a good type, for a Voidbringer.

Darkness turned to the viziers. "I will trouble you no further."

"Mistress!" Wyndle said. "Here!"

The half-eaten roll lay on the floor. She'd dropped it when the cudgel hit. Wyndle ran into it, but he couldn't do anything more than make it wobble. Lift thrashed, trying to pull free, but without that storm inside of her, she was just a child in the grip of a trained soldier.

"I am *highly* disturbed by the nature of this incursion, constable," the lead vizier said, shuffling through the stack of papers that Darkness had dropped. "Your paperwork is in order, and I see you even included a plea—granted by the arbiters—to search the palace itself for this urchin. Surely you did not need to disturb a holy conclave. For a common thief, no less."

"Justice waits upon no man or woman," Darkness said, completely calm. "And this thief is anything but common. With your leave, we will cease disturbing you."

He didn't seem to care if they gave him leave or not. He strode toward the door, and his minion pulled Lift along after. She got her foot out to the roll, but only managed to kick it forward, under the long table by the viziers.

"This is a leave of *execution*," the vizier said with surprise, holding up the last sheet in the stack. "You will kill the child? For mere thievery?"

Kill? *No. No!*

"That, in addition to trespassing in the Prime's palace," Darkness said, reaching the door. "And for interrupting a holy conclave in session."

The vizier met his gaze. She held it, then *wilted*. "I . . ." she said. "Ah, of course . . . er . . . constable."

Darkness turned from her and pulled open the door. The vizier set one hand on the table and raised her other hand to her head.

The minion dragged Lift up to the door.

"Mistress!" Wyndle said, twisting up nearby. "Oh . . . oh dear. There is something very wrong with that man! He is not right, not right at all. You must use your powers."

"Trying," Lift said, grunting.

"You've let yourself grow too thin," Wyndle said. "Not good. You always use up the excess.... Low body fat ... That might be the problem. I don't know *how* this works!"

Darkness hesitated beside the door and looked at the low-hanging chandeliers in the hallway beyond, with their mirrors and sparkling gemstones. He raised his hand and gestured. The minion not holding Lift moved out into the hallway and found the chandelier ropes. He unwound those and pulled, raising the chandeliers.

Lift tried to summon her awesomeness. Just a little more. She just needed a *little*.

Her body felt exhausted. Drained. She really *had* been overdoing it. She struggled, increasingly panicked. Increasingly desperate.

In the hallway, the minion tied off the chandeliers high in the air. Nearby, the vizier leader glanced from Darkness to Lift.

"Please," Lift mouthed.

The vizier pointedly *shoved* the table. It clipped the elbow of the minion holding Lift. He cursed, letting go with that hand.

Lift dove for the floor, ripping out of his grip. She squirmed forward, getting underneath the table.

The minion seized her by the ankles.

"What was that?" Darkness asked, his voice cold, emotionless.

"I slipped," the vizier said.

"Watch yourself."

"Is that a threat, constable? I am beyond your reach."

"Nobody is beyond my reach." Still no emotion.

Lift thrashed underneath the table, kicking at the minion. He cursed softly and hauled Lift out by her legs, then pulled her to her feet. Darkness watched, face emotionless.

She met his gaze, eye to eye, a half-eaten roll in her mouth. She stared him down, chewing quickly and swallowing.

For once, he showed an emotion. Bafflement. "All that," he said, "for a roll?"

Lift said nothing.

Come on . . .

They walked her down the hallway, then around the corner. One of the minions ran ahead and purposefully removed the spheres from the lamps on the walls. Were they *robbing* the place? No, after she passed, the minion ran back and restored the spheres.

Come on . . .

They passed a palace guard in the larger hallway beyond. He noted something about Darkness—perhaps that rope tied around his upper arm, which was threaded with an Azish sequence of colors—and saluted. "Constable, sir? You found another one?"

Darkness stopped, looking as the guard opened the door beside him. Inside, Gawx sat on a chair, slumped between two other guards.

"So you did have accomplices!" shouted one of the guards in the room. He slapped Gawx across the face.

Wyndle gasped from just behind her. "That was *certainly* uncalled for!"

Come on...

"This one is not your concern," Darkness said to the guards, waiting as one of his minions did the strange gemstone-moving sequence. Why *did* they worry about that?

Something stirred inside of Lift. Like the little swirls of wind at the advent of a storm.

Darkness looked at her with a sharp motion. "Something is—"

Awesomeness returned.

Lift became Slick, every part of her but her feet and the palms of her hands. She yanked her arm—it slipped from the minion's fingers—then kicked herself forward and fell to her knees, sliding under Darkness's hand as he reached for her.

Wyndle let out a whoop, zipping along beside her as she began slapping the floor like she was swimming, using each swing of her arms to push herself forward. She skimmed the floor of the palace hallway, knees sliding across it as if it were greased.

The posture wasn't particularly dignified. Dignity was for rich folk who had time to make up games to play with one another.

She got going real fast real quick—so fast it was hard to control herself as she relaxed her awesomeness and tried to leap to her feet. She crashed into the wall at the end of the hallway instead, a sprawling heap of limbs.

She came out of it with a grin. That had gone *way* better than the last few times she'd tried this. Her first attempt had been super embarrassing. She'd been so Slick, she hadn't even been able to stay on her knees.

"Lift!" Wyndle said. "Behind."

She glanced down the hallway. She could *swear* he was glowing faintly, and he was certainly running too quickly.

Darkness was awesome too.

"That is *not* fair!" Lift shouted, scrambling to her feet and dashing down a side hallway—the way she'd come when sneaking with Gawx. Her body had already started to feel tired again. One roll didn't get it far.

She sprinted down the lavish hallway, causing a maid to jump back, shrieking as if she'd seen a rat. Lift skidded around a corner, dashed toward the nice scents, and burst into the kitchens.

She ran through the mess of people inside. The door slammed open behind her a second later. Darkness.

Ignoring startled cooks, Lift leaped up onto a long counter, Slicking her leg and riding on it sideways, knocking off bowls and pans, causing a clatter. She came down off the other end of the counter as Darkness shoved his way past cooks in a clump, his Shardblade held up high.

He didn't curse in annoyance. A fellow should curse. Made people feel real when they did that.

But of course, Darkness wasn't a real person. Of that, though little else, she was sure.

Lift snatched a sausage off a steaming plate, then pushed into the servant hallways. She chewed as she ran, Wyndle growing along the wall beside her, leaving a streak of dark green vines.

"Where are we going?" he asked.

"*Away.*"

The door into the servant hallways slammed open behind her. Lift turned a corner, surprising an equerry. She went awesome, and threw herself to the side, easily slipping past him in the narrow hallway.

"What has become of me?" Wyndle asked. "Thieving

in the night, chased by abominations. I was a gardener. A wonderful gardener! Cryptics and honorspren alike came to see the crystals I grew from the minds of your world. Now this. What *have* I become?"

"A whiner," Lift said, puffing.

"Nonsense."

"So you were always one of those, then?" She looked over her shoulder. Darkness casually shoved down the equerry, barely breaking stride as he charged over the man.

Lift reached a doorway and slammed her shoulder against it, scrambling out into the rich hallways again.

She needed an exit. A window. Her flight had just looped her around back near the Prime's quarters. She picked a direction by instinct and started running, but one of Darkness's minions appeared around a corner that way. He *also* carried a Shardblade. Some starvin' luck, she had.

Lift turned the other way and passed by Darkness striding out of the servant hallways. She barely dodged a swing of his Blade by diving, Slicking herself, and sliding along the floor. She made it to her feet without stumbling this time. That was something, at least.

"Who *are* these men?" Wyndle asked from beside her.

Lift grunted.

"Why do they care so much about you? There's something about those weapons they carry . . ."

"Shardblades," Lift said. "Worth a whole kingdom. Built to kill Voidbringers." And they had *two* of the things. Crazy.

Built to kill Voidbringers . . .

"You!" she said, still running. "They're after you!"

"What? Of course they aren't!"

"They *are*. Don't worry. You're mine. I won't lettem have you."

"That's endearingly loyal," Wyndle said. "And not a little insulting. But they are not after—"

The second of Darkness's minions stepped out into the hallway ahead of her. He held Gawx.

He had a knife to the young man's throat.

Lift stumbled to a halt. Gawx, in far over his head, whimpered in the man's hands.

"Don't move," the minion said, "or I will kill him."

"Starvin' bastard," Lift said. She spat to the side. "That's dirty."

Darkness thumped up behind her, the other minion joining him. They penned her in. The entrance to the Prime's quarters was actually just ahead, and the viziers and scions had flooded out into the hallway, where they jabbered to one another in outraged tones.

Gawx was crying. Poor fool.

Well. This sorta thing never ended well. Lift went

with her gut—which was basically what she always did—and called the minion's bluff by dashing forward. He was a lawman type. Wouldn't kill a captive in cold—

The minion slit Gawx's throat.

Crimson blood poured out and stained Gawx's clothing. The minion dropped him, then stumbled back, as if startled by what he'd done.

Lift froze. He couldn't— He didn't—

Darkness grabbed her from behind.

"That was poorly done," Darkness said to the minion, tone emotionless. Lift barely heard him. *So much blood.* "You will be punished."

"But . . ." the minion said. "I had to do as I threatened . . ."

"You have not done the proper paperwork in this kingdom to kill that child," Darkness said.

"Aren't we above their laws?"

Darkness actually let go of her, striding over to slap the minion across the face. "Without the law, there is nothing. You will subject yourself to their rules, and accept the dictates of justice. It is all we have, the only sure thing in this world."

Lift stared at the dying boy, who held his hands to his neck, as if to stop the blood flow. Those tears . . .

The other minion came up behind her.

"Run!" Wyndle said.

She started.

"*Run!*"

Lift ran.

She passed Darkness and pushed through the viziers, who gasped and yelled at the death. She barreled into the Prime's quarters, slid across the table, snatched another roll off the platter, and burst into the bedroom. She was out the window a second later.

"Up," she said to Wyndle, then stuffed the roll in her mouth. He streaked up the side of the wall, and Lift climbed, sweating. A second later, one of the minions leaped out the window beneath her.

He didn't look up. He charged out onto the grounds, twisting about, searching, his Shardblade flashing in the darkness as it reflected starlight.

Lift safely reached the upper reaches of the palace, hidden in the shadows there. She squatted down, hands around her knees, feeling cold.

"You barely knew him," Wyndle said. "Yet you mourn."

She nodded.

"You've seen much death," Wyndle said. "I know it. Aren't you accustomed to it?"

She shook her head.

Below, the minion moved off, hunting farther and farther for her. She was free. Climb across the roof, slip down on the other side, disappear.

Was that motion on the wall at the edge of the grounds? Yes, those moving shadows were men. The other thieves were climbing their wall and disappearing into the night. Huqin had left his nephew, as expected.

Who would cry for Gawx? Nobody. He'd be forgotten, abandoned.

Lift released her legs and crawled across the curved bulb of the roof toward the window she'd entered earlier. Her vines from the seeds, unlike the ones Wyndle grew, were still alive. They'd overgrown the window, leaves quivering in the wind.

Run, her instincts said. *Go.*

"You spoke of something earlier," she whispered. "Re..."

"Regrowth," he said. "Each bond grants power over two Surges. You can influence how things grow."

"Can I use this to help Gawx?"

"If you were better trained? Yes. As it stands, I doubt it. You aren't very strong, aren't very practiced. And he might be dead already."

She touched one of the vines.

"Why do you care?" Wyndle asked again. He sounded curious. Not a challenge. An attempt to understand.

"Because someone has to."

For once, Lift ignored what her gut was telling her

and, instead, climbed through the window. She crossed the room in a dash.

Out into the upstairs hallway. Onto the steps. She soared down them, leaping most of the distance. Through a doorway. Turn left. Down the hallway. Left again.

A crowd in the rich corridor. Lift reached them, then wiggled through. She didn't need her awesomeness for that. She'd been slipping through cracks in crowds since she started walking.

Gawx lay in a pool of blood that had darkened the fine carpet. The viziers and guards surrounded him, speaking in hushed tones.

Lift crawled up to him. His body was still warm, but the blood seemed to have stopped flowing. His eyes were closed.

"Too late?" she whispered.

"I don't know," Wyndle said, curling up beside her.

"What do I do?"

"I . . . I'm not sure. Mistress, the transition to your side was difficult and left holes in my memory, even with the precautions my people took. I . . ."

She set Gawx on his back, face toward the sky. He *wasn't* really anything to her, that was true. They'd barely just met, and he'd been a fool. She'd told him to go back.

But this was who she was, who she had to be.

I will remember those who have been forgotten.

Lift leaned forward, touched her forehead to his, and breathed out. A shimmering something left her lips, a little cloud of glowing light. It hung in front of Gawx's lips.

Come on . . .

It stirred, then drew in through his mouth.

A hand took Lift by the shoulder, pulling her away from Gawx. She sagged, suddenly exhausted. *Real* exhausted, so much so that even standing was difficult.

Darkness pulled her by the shoulder away from the crowd. "Come," he said.

Gawx stirred. The viziers gasped, their attention turning toward the youth as he groaned, then sat up.

"It appears that you are an Edgedancer," Darkness said, steering her down the corridor as the crowd moved in around Gawx, chattering. She stumbled, but he held her upright. "I had wondered which of the two you would be."

"Miracle!" one vizier said.

"Yaezir has spoken!" said one of the scions.

"Edgedancer," Lift said. "I don't know what that is."

"They were once a glorious order," Darkness said, walking her down the hallway. Everyone ignored them, focused instead on Gawx. "Where you blunder, they were elegant things of beauty. They could ride the thinnest rope at speed, dance across rooftops, move through a battlefield like a ribbon on the wind."

"That sounds . . . amazing."

"Yes. It is unfortunate they were always so concerned with small-minded things, while ignoring those of greater import. It appears you share their temperament. You have become one of them."

"I didn't mean to," Lift said.

"I realize this."

"Why . . . why do you hunt me?"

"In the name of justice."

"There are *tons* of people who do wrong things," she said. She had to force out every word. Talking was hard. *Thinking* was hard. So tired. "You . . . you coulda hunted big crime bosses, murderers. You chose me instead. Why?"

"Others may be detestable, but they do not dabble in arts that could return Desolation to this world." His words were so cold. "What you are must be stopped."

Lift felt numb. She tried to summon her awesomeness, but she'd used it all up. And then some, probably.

Darkness turned her and pushed her against the wall. She couldn't stand, and slumped down, sitting. Wyndle moved up beside her, spreading out a starburst of creeping vines.

Darkness knelt next to her. He held out his hand.

"I *saved* him," Lift said. "I did something good, didn't I?"

"Goodness is irrelevant," Darkness said. His Shardblade dropped into his fingers.

"You don't even care, do you?"

"No," he said. "I don't."

"You should," she said, exhausted. "You should . . . should try it, I mean. I wanted to be like you, once. Didn't work out. Wasn't . . . even like being alive . . ."

Darkness raised his Blade.

Lift closed her eyes.

"She is pardoned!"

Darkness's grip on her shoulder tightened.

Feeling completely drained—like somebody had held her up by the toes and squeezed everything out of her—Lift forced her eyes to open. Gawx stumbled to a stop beside them, breathing heavily. Behind, the viziers and scions moved up as well.

Clothing bloodied, his eyes wide, Gawx clutched a piece of paper in his hand. He thrust this at Darkness. "I pardon this girl. Release her, constable!"

"Who are you," Darkness said, "to do such a thing?"

"I am the Prime Aqasix," Gawx declared. "Ruler of Azir!"

"Ridiculous."

"The Kadasixes have spoken," said one of the scions.

"The Heralds?" Darkness said. "They have done no such thing. You are mistaken."

"We have voted," said a vizier. "This young man's application was the best."

"What application?" Darkness said. "He is a thief!"

"He performed the miracle of Regrowth," said one of the older scions. "He was dead and he returned. What better application could we ask for?"

"A sign has been given," said the lead vizier. "We have a Prime who can survive the attacks of the One All White. Praise to Yaezir, Kadasix of Kings, may he lead in wisdom. This youth is Prime. He has *been* Prime always. We have only now realized it, and beg his forgiveness for not seeing the truth sooner."

"As it always has been done," the elderly scion said. "As it will be done again. Stand down, constable. You have been given an order."

Darkness studied Lift.

She smiled tiredly. Show the starvin' man some teeth. That was the right of it.

His Shardblade vanished to mist. He'd been bested, but he didn't seem to care. Not a curse, not even a tightening of the eyes. He stood up and pulled on his gloves by the cuffs, first one, then the other. "Praise Yaezir," he said. "Herald of Kings. May he lead in wisdom. If he ever stops drooling."

Darkness bowed to the new Prime, then left with a sure step.

"Does anyone know the name of that constable?" one of the viziers asked. "When did we start letting officers of the law requisition Shardblades?"

Gawx knelt beside Lift.

"So you're an emperor or something now," she said, closing her eyes, settling back.

"Yeah. I'm still confused. It seems I performed a miracle or something."

"Good for you," Lift said. "Can I eat your dinner?"

1

Lift prepared to be awesome.

She sprinted across an open field in northern Ta-shikk, a little more than a week's travel from Azimir. The place was overgrown with brown grass a foot or two high. The occasional trees were tall and twisty, with trunks that looked like they were made of inter-woven vines, and branches that pointed upward more than out.

They had some official name, but everyone she knew called them drop-deads because of their springy roots. In a storm, they'd fall over flat and just lie there. Afterward they'd pop back up, like a rude gesture made at the passing winds.

Lift's run startled a group of axehinds who had been grazing nearby; the lean creatures leaped away on four legs with the two front claws pulled in close to the body. Good eating, those beasties. Barely any shell on them. But for once, Lift wasn't in the mood to eat.

She was on the *run*.

"Mistress!" Wyndle, her pet Voidbringer, called. He took the shape of a vine, growing along the ground beside her at superfast speed, matching her pace. He didn't have a face at the moment, but could speak anyway. Unfortunately.

"Mistress," he pled, "can't we please just *go back*?"

Nope.

Lift became awesome. She drew on the stuff inside of her, the stuff that made her glow. She Slicked the soles of her feet with it, and leaped into a skid.

Suddenly, the ground didn't rub against her at all. She slid as if on ice, whipping through the field. Grass startled all around her, curling as it yanked down into stone burrows. That made it bow before her in a wave.

She zipped along, wind pushing back her long black hair, tugging at the loose overshirt she wore atop her tighter brown undershirt, which was tucked into her loose-cuffed trousers.

She slid, and felt free. Just her and the wind. A small windspren, like a white ribbon in the air, started to follow her.

Then she hit a rock.

The stupid rock held firm—it was held in place by little tufts of moss that grew on the ground and stuck to things like stones, holding them down as shelter against the wind. Lift's foot flashed with pain and she tumbled in the air, then hit the stone ground face-first.

Reflexively, she made her face awesome—so she kept right on going, skidding on her cheek until she hit a tree. She stopped there, finally.

The tree slowly fell over, playing dead. It hit the ground with a shivering sound of leaves and branches.

Lift sat up, rubbing her face. She'd cut her foot, but her awesomeness plugged up the hole, healing it plenty quick. Her face didn't even hurt much. When a part of her was awesome, it didn't rub on what it touched, it just kind of . . . glided.

She still felt stupid.

"Mistress," Wyndle said, curling up to her. His vine looked like the type fancy people would grow on their buildings to hide up parts that didn't look rich enough. Except he had bits of crystal growing out of him along the vine's length. They jutted out unexpectedly, like toenails on a face.

When he moved, he didn't wiggle like an eel. He actually grew, leaving a long trail of vines behind him that would soon crystallize and decay into dust. Voidbringers were strange.

He wound around himself in a circle, like rope coiling, and formed a small tower of vines. And then something grew from the top: a face that formed out of vines, leaves, and gemstones. The mouth worked as he spoke.

"Oh, mistress," he said. "Can't we stop playing out here, *please*? We need to get back to Azimir!"

"Go back?" Lift stood up. "We just escaped that place!"

"Escaped! The *palace*? Mistress, you were an honored guest of the emperor! You had everything you wanted, as much food, as much—"

"All lies," she declared, hands on hips. "To keep me from noticin' the truth. They was going to *eat* me."

Wyndle stammered. He wasn't so frightening, for a Voidbringer. He must have been like . . . the Voidbringer all the other ones made fun of for wearing silly hats. The one that would correct all the others, and explain which fork they had to use when they sat down to consume human souls.

"Mistress," Wyndle said. "Humans do *not* eat other humans. You were a guest!"

"Yeah, but *why*? They gave me too much stuff."

"You saved the emperor's life!"

"That should've been good for a few days of free-loading," she said. "I once pulled a guy out of prison, and he gave me five whole days in his den for free, and a nice handkerchief too. *That* was generous. The Azish letting me stay as long as I wanted?" She shook her head. "They wanted something. Only explanation. They was going to starvin' eat me."

"But—"

Lift started running again. The cold stone, perforated by grass burrows, felt good on her toes and feet. No shoes. What good were shoes? In the palace, they'd started offering her heaps of shoes. And nice clothing—big, comfy coats and robes. Clothing you could get lost in. She'd liked wearing something soft for once.

Then they'd started asking. Why not take some lessons, and learn to read? They were grateful for what she'd done for Gawx, who was now Prime Aqasix, a fancy title for their ruler. Because of her service, she could have tutors, they said. She could learn how to wear those clothes properly, learn how to write.

It had started to consume her. If she'd stayed, how long would it have been before she wasn't Lift anymore? How long until she'd have been gobbled up, another girl left in her place? Similar face, but at the same time all new?

She tried using her awesomeness again. In the palace, they had talked about the recovery of ancient powers. Knights Radiant. The binding of Surges, natural forces.

I will remember those who have been forgotten.

Lift Slicked herself with power, then skidded across

the ground a few feet before tumbling and rolling through the grass.

She pounded her fist on the stones. Stupid ground. Stupid awesomeness. How was she supposed to stay standing, when her feet were slipperier than if they'd been coated in oil? She should just go back to paddling around on her knees. It was so much easier. She could balance that way, and use her hands to steer. Like a little crab, scooting around this way and that.

They were elegant things of beauty, Darkness had said. *They could ride the thinnest rope, dance across rooftops, move like a ribbon on the wind....*

Darkness, the shadow of a man who had chased her, had said those things in the palace, speaking of those who had—long ago—used powers like Lift's. Maybe he'd been lying. After all, he'd been preparing to murder her at the time.

Then again, why lie? He'd treated her derisively, as if she were nothing. Worthless.

She set her jaw and stood up. Wyndle was still talking, but she ignored him, instead taking off across the deserted field, running as fast as she could, startling grass. She reached the top of a small hill, then jumped and coated her feet with power.

She started slipping immediately. The air. The air she pushed against when moving was holding her back. Lift hissed, then coated her *entire self* in power.

She sliced through the wind, turning sideways as she skidded down the side of the hill. Air slid off her, as if it couldn't find her. Even the sunlight seemed to melt off her skin. She was between places, here but not. No air, no ground. Just pure motion, so fast that she reached grass before it had time to pull away. It flowed around her, its touch brushed aside by her power.

Her skin started to glow, tendrils of smoky light rising from her. She laughed, reaching the bottom of the small hill. There she leaped some boulders.

And ran face-first into another tree.

The bubble of power around her popped. The tree toppled over—and, for good measure, the two next to it decided to fall as well. Perhaps they thought they were missing out on something.

Wyndle found her grinning like a fool, staring up at the sun, spread out on the tree trunk with her arms interwoven with the branches, a single golden gloryspren—shaped like an orb—circling above her.

"Mistress?" he said. "Oh, mistress. You were *happy* in the palace. I saw it in you!"

She didn't reply.

"And the emperor," Wyndle continued. "He'll miss you! You didn't even tell him you were going!"

"I left him a note."

"A note? You learned to write?"

"Storms, no. I ate his dinner. Right out from under the tray cover while they was preparing to bring it to him. Gawx'll know what that means."

"I find that doubtful, mistress."

She climbed up from the fallen tree and stretched, then blew her hair out of her eyes. Maybe she *could* dance across rooftops, ride on ropes, or . . . what was it? Make wind? Yeah, she could do that one for sure. She hopped off the tree and continued walking through the field.

Unfortunately, her stomach had a few things to say about how much awesomeness she'd used. She ran on food, even more than most folks. She could draw some awesomeness from everything she ate, but once it was gone, she couldn't do anything incredible again until she'd had more to eat.

Her stomach rumbled in complaint. She liked to imagine that it was cussing at her something awful, and she searched through her pockets. She'd run out of the food in her pack—she'd taken a *lot*—this morning. But hadn't she found a sausage in the bottom before tossing the pack?

Oh, right. She'd eaten that while watching those riverspren a few hours ago. She dug in her pockets anyway, but only came out with a handkerchief that she'd used to wrap up a big stack of flatbread before

stuffing it in her pack. She shoved part of the handkerchief into her mouth and started chewing.

"Mistress?" Wyndle asked.

"Mie hab crubs onnit," she said around the
handkerchief.

"You shouldn't have been Surgebinding so much!"
He wound along on the ground beside her, leaving a
trail of vines and crystals. "And we *should* have stayed
in the palace. Oh, how did this happen to me? I should
be gardening right now. I had the most *magnificent*
chairs."

"Shars?" Lift asked, pausing.

"Yes, chairs." Wyndle wound up in a coil beside her,
forming a face that tilted toward her at an angle off
the top of the coil. "While in Shadesmar, I had col-
lected the most magnificent selection of the souls of
chairs from your side! I cultivated them, grew them
into grand crystals. I had some Winstels, a nice Shober,
quite the collection of spoonbacks, even a throne or
two!"

"Yu gurdened *shars*?"

"Of course I gardened chairs," Wyndle said. His ribbon of vine leaped off the coil and followed her as she
started walking again. "What else would I garden?"

"Fwants."

"Plants? Well, we have them in Shadesmar, but I'm

no *pedestrian* gardener. I'm an artist! Why, I was planning an entire exhibition of sofas when the Ring chose me for this atrocious duty."

"Smufld gramitch mragnifude."

"Would you take that out of your mouth?" Wyndle snapped.

Lift did so.

Wyndle huffed. How a little vine thing huffed, Lift didn't know. But he did it all the time. "Now, what were you trying to say?"

"Gibberish," Lift said. "I just wanted to see how you'd respond." She stuffed the other side of the handkerchief into her mouth and started sucking on it.

They continued on with a sigh from Wyndle, who muttered about gardening and his pathetic life. He certainly was a strange Voidbringer. Come to think of it, she'd never seen him act the least bit interested in consuming someone's soul. Maybe he was a vegetarian?

They passed through a small forest, really just a corpse of trees, which was a strange term, since she never seemed to find any bodies in them. These weren't even drop-deads; those tended to grow in small patches, but each apart from the others. These had branches that wound around one another as they grew, dense and intertwined to face the highstorms.

That was basically the way to do it, right? Everyone else, they wound their branches together. Braced themselves. But Lift, she was a drop-dead. Don't intertwine, don't get caught up. Go your own way.

Yes, that was definitely how she was. That was why she'd had to leave the palace, obviously. You couldn't live your life getting up and seeing the same things every day. You had to keep moving, otherwise people started to know who you were, and then they started to expect things from you. It was one step from there to being gobbled up.

She stopped right inside the trees, standing on a pathway that someone had cut and kept maintained. She looked backward, northward, toward Azir.

"Is this about what happened to you?" Wyndle asked. "I don't know a lot about humans, but I *believe* it was natural, disconcerting though it might appear. You aren't wounded."

Lift shaded her eyes. The wrong things were changing. She was supposed to stay the same, and the world was supposed to change around her. She'd asked for that, hadn't she?

Had she been lied to?

"Are we . . . going back?" Wyndle asked, hopeful.

"No," Lift said. "Just saying goodbye." Lift shoved her hands in her pockets and turned around before continuing through the trees.

2

Yeddaw was one of those cities Lift had always meant to visit. It was in Tashikk, a strange place even compared to Azir. She'd always found everyone here too polite and reserved. They also wore clothing that made them hard to read.

But everyone said that you had to see Yeddaw. It was the closest you could get to seeing Sesemalex Dar—and considering *that* place had been a war zone for basically a billion years, she wasn't likely to ever get there.

Standing with hands on hips, looking down at the city of Yeddaw, she found herself agreeing with what people said. This *was* a sight. The Azish liked to consider themselves grand, but they only plastered bronze or gold or something over all their buildings and pretended that was enough. What good did that do? It just reflected her own face at her, and she'd seen that too often to be impressed by it.

No, *this* was impressive. A majestic city cut *out of the starvin' ground.*

She'd heard some of the fancy scribes in Azir talk about it—they said it was a new city, created only a hunnerd years back by hiring the Imperial Shardblades out of Azir. Those didn't spend much time at war, but were instead used for making mines or cutting up rocks and stuff. Very practical. Like using the royal throne as a stool to reach something on the high shelf.

She really shouldn't have gotten yelled at for that.

Anyway, they'd used those Shardblades here. This had once been a large, flat plain. Her vantage on a hilltop, though, let her make out hundreds of trenches cut in the stone. They interconnected, like a huge maze. Some of the trenches were wider than others, and they made a vague spiral toward the center, where a large moundlike building was the only part of the city that peeked up over the surface of the plain.

Above, in the spaces between trenches, people worked fields. There were virtually no structures up there; everything was down below. People *lived* in those trenches, which seemed to be two or three stories deep. How did they avoid being washed away in highstorms? True, they'd cut large channels leading out from the city—ones nobody seemed to live in, so the water could escape. Still didn't seem safe, but it *was* pretty cool.

She could hide really well in there. That was why she'd come, after all. To hide. Nothing else. No other reason.

The city didn't have walls, but it did have a number of guard towers spaced around it. Her pathway led down from the hills and joined with a larger road, which eventually stopped in a line of people awaiting permission to get into the city.

"How on Roshar did they manage to cut away so much rock!" Wyndle said, forming a pile of vines beside her, a twisting column that took him high enough to be by her waist, face tilted toward the city.

"Shardblades," Lift said.

"Oh. Ooooh. Those." He shifted uncomfortably, vines writhing and twisting about one another with a scrunching sound. "Yes. Those."

She folded her arms. "I should get me one of those, eh?"

Wyndle, strangely, groaned loudly.

"I figure," she explained, "that Darkness has one, right? He fought with one when he was trying to kill me and Gawx. So I ought to find one."

"Yes," Wyndle said, "you should do just that! Let us pop over to the market and pick up a legendary, all-powerful weapon of myth and lore, worth more than many kingdoms! I hear they sell them in bushels, following spring weather in the east."

"Shut it, Voidbringer." She eyed his tangle of a face. "You know something about Shardblades, don't you?"

The vines seemed to wilt.

"You *do*. Out with it. What do you know?"

He shook his vine head.

"Tell me," Lift warned.

"It's forbidden. You must discover it on your own."

"That's what I'm doing. I'm discovering it. From you. Tell me, or I'll *bite* you."

"*What?*"

"I'll bite you," she said. "I'll gnaw on you, Voidbringer. You're a vine, right? I eat plants. Sometimes."

"Even assuming my crystals wouldn't break your teeth," Wyndle said, "my mass would give you no sustenance. It would break down into dust."

"It's not about sustenance. It's about torture."

Wyndle, surprisingly, met her expression with his strange eyes grown from crystals. "Honestly, mistress, I don't think you have it in you."

She growled at him, and he wilted further, but didn't tell her the secret. Well, storms. It was good to see him have a backbone . . . or, well, the plant equivalent, whatever that was. Backbark?

"You're supposed to obey me," she said, shoving her hands in her pockets and heading along the path toward the city. "You ain't following the rules."

"I am indeed," he said with a huff. "You just don't know them. And I'll have you know that I am a gardener, and not a soldier, so I'll *not* have you hitting people with me."

She stopped. "Why would I hit anyone with you?"

He wilted so far, he was practically shriveled.

Lift sighed, then continued on her way, Wyndle following. They merged with the larger road, turning toward the tower that was a gateway into the city.

"So," Wyndle said as they passed a chull cart, "this is where we were going all along? This city cut into the ground?"

Lift nodded.

"You could have told me," Wyndle said. "I've been worried we'd be caught outside in a storm!"

"Why? It ain't raining anymore." The Weeping, oddly, had stopped. Then started again. Then stopped again. It was acting downright strange, like regular weather, rather than the long, long mild highstorm it was supposed to be.

"I don't know," Wyndle said. "Something is wrong, mistress. Something in the world. I can feel it. Did you hear what the Alethi king wrote to the emperor?"

"About a new storm coming?" Lift said. "One that blows the wrong way?"

"Yes."

"The noodles all called that silly."

"Noodles?"

"The people who hang around Gawx, talking to him all the time, telling him what to do and trying to get me to wear a robe."

"The *viziers* of *Azir*. Head clerks of the empire and advisors to the Prime!"

"Yeah. Wavy arms and blubbering features. Noodles. Anyway, they thought that angry guy—"

"—Highprince Dalinar Kholin, de facto king of Alethkar and most powerful warlord in the world right now—"

"—was makin' stuff up."

"Maybe. But don't you feel something? Out there? Building?"

"A distant thunder," Lift whispered, looking westward, past the city, toward the far-off mountains. "Or . . . or the way you feel after someone drops a pan, and you see it falling, and get ready for the clatter it will make when it hits."

"So you do feel it."

"Maybe," Lift said. The chull cart rolled past. Nobody paid any attention to her—they never did. And nobody could see Wyndle but her, because *she* was *special.* "Don't your Voidbringer friends know about this?"

"We're not . . . Lift, we're spren, but my kind—cultivationspren—are not very important. We don't have a kingdom, or even cities, of our own. We only moved to bond with you because the Cryptics and the honorspren and everyone were starting to move. Oh, we've jumped *right* into the sea of glass feet-first, but we barely know what we're doing! Everyone who had any idea of how to accomplish all this died centuries ago!"

He grew along the road beside her as they followed the chull cart, which rattled and shook as it bounced down the roadway.

"Everything is wrong, and nothing makes sense," Wyndle continued. "Bonding to you was supposed to be more difficult than it was, I gather. Memories come to me fuzzily sometimes, but I do remember more and more. I didn't go through the trauma we all thought I'd endure. That might be because of your . . . unique circumstances. But mistress, listen to me when I say something big is coming. This was the wrong time to leave Azir. We were secure there. We'll need security."

"There isn't time to get back."

"No. There probably isn't. At least we have shelter ahead."

"Yeah. Assuming Darkness doesn't kill us."

"Darkness? The Skybreaker who attacked you in the palace and came very close to murdering you?"

"Yeah," Lift said. "He's in the city. Didn't you hear me complaining that I needed a Shardblade?"

"In the city . . . in Yeddaw, where we're *going right now*?"

"Yup. The noodles have people watching for reports of him. A note came in right before we left, saying he'd been spotted in Yeddaw."

"Wait." Wyndle zipped forward, leaving a trail of vines and crystal behind. He grew up the back of the chull cart, curling onto its wood right in front of her. He made a face there, looking at her. "Is *that* why we left all of a sudden? Is *that* why we're here? Did you come *chasing* that monster?"

"Course not," Lift said, hands in her pockets. "That would be stupid."

"Which you are not."

"Nope."

"Then *why* are we *here*?"

"They got these pancakes here," she said, "with things cooked into them. Supposed to be super tasty, and they eat them during the Weeping. Ten varieties. I'm gonna steal one of each."

"You came all this way, leaving behind luxury, to eat some pancakes."

"Really *awesome* pancakes."

"Despite the fact that a deific Shardbearer is here—a man who went to great lengths to try to execute you."

"He wanted to stop me from using my powers," Lift said. "He's been seen other places. The noodles looked into it; they're fascinated by him. Everyone pays attention to that bald guy who collects the heads of kings, but *this* guy has been murdering his way across Roshar too. Little people. Quiet people."

"And we came here why?"

She shrugged. "Seemed like as good a place as any."

He let himself slide off the back of the cart. "As a point of fact, it most expressly is *not* as good a place as any. It is demonstrably worse for—"

"You sure I can't eat you?" she asked. "That would be super convenient. You got lots of extra vines. Maybe I could nibble on a few of those."

"I assure you, mistress, that you would find the experience *thoroughly* unappealing."

She grunted, stomach growling. Hungerspren appeared, like little brown specks with wings, floating around her. That wasn't odd. Many of the folks in line had attracted them.

"I got two powers," Lift said. "I can slide around, awesome, and I can make stuff grow. So I could grow me some plants to eat?"

"It would almost certainly take more energy in

Stormlight to grow the plants than the sustenance would provide, as determined by the laws of the universe. And before you say anything, these are laws that even *you* cannot ignore." He paused. "I think. Who knows, when *you're* involved?"

"I'm *special*," Lift said, stopping as they finally reached the line of people waiting to get into the city. "Also, hungry. More hungry than special, right now."

She poked her head out of the line. Several guards stood at the ramp down into the city, along with some scribes wearing the odd Tashikki clothing. It was this *loooong* piece of cloth that they wrapped around themselves, feet to forehead. For being a single sheet, it was really complex: it wound around both legs and arms individually, but also wrapped back around the waist sometimes to create a kind of skirt. Both the men and the women wore the cloths, though not the guards.

They sure were taking their time letting people in. And there sure were a lot of people waiting. Everyone here was Makabaki, with dark eyes and skin—darker than Lift's brownish tan. And a lot of those waiting were families, wearing normal Azish-style clothing. Trousers, dirty skirts, some with patterns. They buzzed with exhaustionspren and hungerspren, enough to be distracting.

She'd have expected mostly merchants, not families, to be waiting here. Who were all these people?

Her stomach growled.

"Mistress?" Wyndle asked.

"Hush," she said. "Too hungry to talk."

"Are you—"

"Hungry? Yes. So shut up."

"But—"

"I bet those guards have food. People always feed guards. They can't properly hit folks on the head if they're starvin'. That's a *fact*."

"Or, to offer a counterproposal, you could simply *buy* some food with the spheres the emperor allotted you."

"Didn't bring them."

"You didn't . . . you didn't *bring the money*?"

"Ditched it when you weren't looking. Can't get robbed if you don't have money. Carrying spheres is just asking for trouble. Besides." She narrowed her eyes, watching the guards. "Only fancy people have money like that. We normal folk, we have to get by some other way."

"So now you're normal."

"Course I am," she said. "It's everyone else that's weird."

Before he could reply, she ducked underneath the chull wagon and started sneaking toward the front of the line.

3

"Tallew, you say?" Hauka asked, holding up the tarp covering the suspicious pile of grain. "From Azir?"

"Yes, of course, officer." The man sitting on the front of the wagon squirmed. "Just a humble farmer."

With no calluses, Hauka thought. *A humble farmer who can afford fine Liaforan boots and a silk belt.* Hauka took her spear and started shoving it into the grain, blunt end first. She didn't run across any contraband, or any refugees, hidden in the grain. So that was a first.

"I need to get your papers notarized," she said. "Pull your cart over to the side here."

The man grumbled but obeyed, turning his cart and starting to back the chull into the spot beside the guard post. It was one of the only buildings erected here above the city, along with a few towers spaced where they could lob arrows at anyone trying to use the ramps or set up position to siege.

The farmer with the wagon backed his cart in very, very carefully—as they were near the ledge overlooking the city. Immigrant quarter. Rich people didn't enter here, only the ones without papers. Or the ones who hoped to avoid scrutiny.

Hauka rolled up the man's credentials and walked past the guard post. Scents wafted out of that; lunch was being set up, which meant the people in line had an even longer wait ahead of them. An old scribe sat in a seat near the front of the guard post. Nissiqqan liked to be out in the sun.

Hauka bowed to him; Nissiqqan was the deputy scribe of immigration on duty for today. The older man was wrapped head-to-toe in a yellow shiqua, though he'd pulled the face portion down to expose a furrowed face with a cleft chin. They were in home lands, and the need to cover up before Nun Raylisi—the enemy of their god—was minimal. Tashi supposedly protected them here.

Hauka herself wore a breastplate, cap, trousers, and a cloak with her family and studies pattern on them. The locals accepted an Azish like her with ease—Tashikk didn't have much in the way of its own soldiers, and her credentials of achievement were certified by an Azimir vizier. She could have gotten a similar officer's job with the local guard anywhere in the greater Makabaki region, though her credentials *did* make clear she wasn't certified for battlefield command.

"Captain?" Nissiqqan said, adjusting his spectacles and looking at the farmer's credentials as she proffered them. "Is he refusing to pay the tariff?"

"Tariff is fine and in the strongbox," Hauka said. "I'm suspicious though. That man's no farmer."

"Smuggling refugees?"

"Checked in the grain and under the cart," Hauka said, looking over her shoulder. The man was all smiles. "It's new grain. A little overripe, but edible."

"Then the city will be glad to have it."

He was right. The war between Emul and Tukar was heating up. Granted, everyone was always saying that. But things *had* changed over the last few years. That god-king of the Tukari . . . there were all sorts of wild rumors about him.

"That's it!" Hauka said. "Your Grace, I'll bet that man has been in Emul. He's been raiding their fields while all the able-bodied men are fighting the invasion."

Nissiqqan nodded in agreement, rubbing his chin. Then he dug through his folder. "Tax him as a smuggler *and* as a fence. I believe . . . yes, that will work. Triple tariff. I'll earmark the extra tariffs to be diverted to feeding refugees, per referendum three-seventy-one-sha."

"Thanks," Hauka said, relaxing and taking the forms. Say what you would of the strange clothing and religion of the Tashikki, they certainly did know how to draft solid civil ordinances.

"I have spheres for you," Nissiqqan noted. "I know you've been asking for infused ones."

"Really!" Hauka said.

"My cousin had some out in his sphere cage—pure luck that he'd forgotten them—when that unpredicted highstorm blew through."

"Excellent," Hauka said. "I'll trade you for them later." She had some information that Nissiqqan would be very interested in. They used that as currency here in Tashikk, as much as they did spheres.

And storms, some lit spheres would be nice. After the Weeping, most people didn't have any, which could be storming inconvenient—as open flame was forbidden in the city. So she couldn't do any reading at night unless she found some infused spheres.

She walked back to the smuggler, flipping through forms. "We'll need you to pay this tariff," she said, handing him a form. "And then this one too."

"A fencing permit!" the man exclaimed. "And smuggling! This is thievery!"

"Yes, I believe it is. Or was."

"You can't prove such allegations," he said, slapping the forms with his hand.

"Sure," she said. "If I could *prove* that you crossed the border into Emul illegally, robbed the fields of good hardworking people while they were distracted by the fighting, then carted it here without proper permits, I'd simply seize the whole thing." She leaned in. "You're getting off easily. We both know it."

He met her eyes, then looked nervously away and started filling out the forms. Good. No trouble today. She liked it when there was no trouble. It—

Hauka stopped. The tarp on the man's wagon was rustling. Frowning, Hauka whipped it backward, and found a young *girl* neck-deep in the grain. She had light brown skin—like she was Reshi, or maybe Herdazian—and was probably eleven or twelve years old. She grinned at Hauka.

She hadn't been there before.

"This stuff," the girl said in Azish, mouth full of what appeared to be uncooked grain, "tastes terrible. I guess that's why we make stuff out of it first." She swallowed. "Got anything to drink?"

The smuggler stood up on his cart, sputtering and

pointing. "She's ruining my goods! She's *swimming* in it! Guard, do something! There's a dirty refugee in my *grain*!"

Great. The paperwork on this was going to be a nightmare. "Out of there, child. Do you have parents?"

"Course I do," the girl said, rolling her eyes. "Everyone's got parents. Mine'r' dead though." She cocked her head. "What's that I smell? That wouldn't be ... pancakes, would it?"

"Sure," Hauka said, sensing an opportunity. "Sun Day pancakes. You can have one, if you—"

"Thanks!" The girl leaped from the grain, spraying it in all directions, causing the smuggler to cry out. Hauka tried to snatch the child, but somehow the girl wiggled out of her grip. She leaped over Hauka's hands, then bounded forward.

And landed right on Hauka's shoulders.

Hauka grunted at the sudden weight of the girl, who jumped off her shoulders and landed behind her.

Hauka spun about, off-balance.

"Tashi!" the smuggler said. "She stepped on your *storming shoulders,* officer."

"Thank you. Stay here. Don't move." Hauka straightened her cap, then dashed after the child, who brushed past Nissiqqan—causing him to drop his folders—and entered into the guard chamber. Good. There weren't any other ways out of that post. Hauka stumbled up to the doorway, setting aside her spear and taking the club from her belt. She didn't want to hurt the little refugee, but some intimidation wouldn't be out of order.

The girl slid across the wooden floor as if it were covered in oil, passing right under the table where several scribes and two of Hauka's guards were eating. The girl then stood up and knocked the entire thing on its side, startling everyone backward and dumping food to the floor.

"Sorry!" the girl called from the mess. "Didn't mean to do that." Her head popped up from beside the overturned table, and she had a pancake sticking half out of her mouth. "These aren't bad."

Hauka's men leaped to their feet. Hauka lunged past them, trying to reach around the table to grab the refugee. Her fingers brushed the arm of the girl, who wiggled away again. The child pushed against the floor and slid right between Rez's legs.

Hauka lunged again, cornering the girl on the side of the guard chamber.

The girl, in turn, reached up and wiggled through the room's single slotlike window. Hauka gaped. Surely that wasn't big enough for a person, even a small one, to get through so easily. She pressed herself against the wall, looking out the window. She didn't see anything at first; then the girl's head poked down from above—she'd gotten onto the roof somehow.

The girl's dark hair blew in the breeze. "Hey," she said. "What kind of pancake *was* that, anyway? I've gotta eat all ten."

"Get back in here," Hauka said, reaching through to try to grab the girl. "You haven't been processed for immigration."

The girl's head popped back upward, and her footsteps sounded on the roof. Hauka cursed and scrambled out the front, trailed by her two guards. They searched the roof of the small guard post, but saw nothing.

"She's back in here!" one of the scribes called from inside.

A moment later, the girl skidded out along the ground, a pancake in each hand and another in her mouth. She passed the guards and scrambled toward the cart with the smuggler, who had climbed down and was ranting about his grain getting soiled.

Hauka leaped to grab the child—and this time managed to get hold of her leg. Unfortunately, her two guards reached for the girl too, and they tripped, falling in a jumbled mess right on top of Hauka.

She hung on though. Puffing from the weight on her back, Hauka clung tightly to the little girl's leg. She looked up, holding in a groan.

The refugee girl sat on the stone in front of her, head cocked. She stuffed one of the pancakes into her mouth, then reached behind herself, her hand darting toward the hitch where the cart was hooked to its chull. The hitch came undone, the hook popping out as the girl tapped it on the bottom. It didn't resist a bit.

Oh, storms no.

"Off me!" Hauka screamed, letting go of the girl and pushing free of the men. The stupid smuggler backed away, confused.

The cart rolled toward the ledge behind, and she doubted the wooden fence would keep it from falling. Hauka leaped for the cart in a burst of energy, seizing it by its side. It dragged her along with it, and she had terrible visions of it plummeting down over the ledge into the city, right on top of the refugees of the immigrant quarter.

The cart, however, slowly lurched to a halt. Puffing, Hauka looked up from where she stood, feet pressed against the stones, holding onto the cart. She didn't dare let go.

The girl was there, on top of the grain again, eating the last pancake. "They really are good."

"Tuk-cake," Hauka said, feeling exhausted. "You eat them for prosperity in the year to come."

"People should eat them all the time then, you know?"

"Maybe."

The girl nodded, then stood to the side and kicked open the tailgate of the cart. In a rush, the grain *slid* out of the cart.

It was the strangest thing she'd ever seen. The pile of grain became like liquid, flowing out of the cart even though the incline was shallow. It ... well, it *glowed* softly as it flowed out and rained down into the city.

The girl smiled at Hauka.

Then she jumped off after it.

Hauka gaped as the girl fell after the grain. The two other guards finally woke up enough to come help, and grabbed hold of the cart. The smuggler was screaming, angerspren boiling up around him like pools of blood on the ground.

Below, the grain billowed in the air, sending up dust as it poured into the immigrant quarter. It was rather far down, but Hauka was pretty sure she heard shouts of delight and praise as the food blanketed the people there.

Cart secure, Hauka stepped up to the ledge. The girl was nowhere to be seen. Storms. Had she been some kind of spren? Hauka searched again but saw nothing, though there was this strange black dust at her feet. It blew away in the wind.

"Captain?" Rez asked.

"Take over immigration for the next hour, Rez. I need a break."

Storms. How on Roshar was she ever going to explain *this* in a report?

4

Lift wasn't supposed to be able to touch Wyndle. The Voidbringer kept saying things like "I don't have enough presence in this Realm, even with our bond" and "you must be stuck partially in the Cognitive." Gibberish, basically.

Because she *could* touch him. That was very useful at times. Times like when you'd just jumped off a short cliff, and needed something to hold on to. Wyndle yelped in surprise as she leaped, then he immediately shot down the side of the wall, moving faster than she fell. He was finally learning to pay attention.

Lift grabbed ahold of him like a rope, one that she halfway held to as she fell, the vine sliding between her fingers. It wasn't much, but it did help slow her descent. She hit harder than would have been safe for most people. Fortunately, she was awesome.

She extinguished the glow of her awesomeness,

then dashed to a small alleyway. People crowded around behind her, praising various Heralds and gods for the gift of the grain. Well, they could speak like that if they wanted, but they all seemed to know the grain hadn't come from a god—not directly—because it was snatched up quicker than a pretty whore in Bavland.

In minutes, all that was left of an entire cartload of grain was a few husks blowing in the wind. Lift settled in the alleyway's mouth, inspecting her surroundings. It was like she'd dropped from noonday straight into dusk. Long shadows everywhere, and things smelled wet.

The buildings were cut right into the stone—doorways, windows, and everything bored out of the rock. They painted the walls these bright colors, often in columns to differentiate one "building" from another. People swarmed all about, chatting and stomping and coughing.

This was the good kind of life. Lift liked being on the move, but she didn't like being alone. Solitary was different from alone. She stood up and started walking, hands in pockets, trying to look in all directions at once. This place was amazing.

"That was quite generous of you, mistress," Wyndle said, growing along beside her. "Dumping that grain, after hearing that the man who had it was a thief."

"That?" Lift said. "I just wanted something soft to land on if you were snoozing."

The people she passed wore a variety of attire. Mostly Azish patterns or Tashikki shiquas. But some were mercenaries, probably either Tukari or Emuli. Others wore rural clothing with a lighter coloring, probably from Alm or Desh. She liked those places. Few people had tried to kill her in Alm or Desh.

Unfortunately, there wasn't much to steal there—unless you liked eating mush, and this strange meat they put in everything. It came from some beast that lived on the mountain slopes, an ugly thing with dirty hair all over it. Lift thought they tasted disgusting, and *she'd* once tried to eat a *roofing tile.*

Anyway, on this street there seemed to be far fewer Tashikki than there were foreigners—but what had they called this above? Immigrant quarter? Well, she probably wouldn't stick out here. She even passed a few Reshi, though most of these were huddled near alleyway shanties, wearing little more than rags.

That was an oddity about this place, for sure. It had shanties. She hadn't seen those since leaving Zawfix, which had them inside of old mines. Most places, if people tried to build homes out of shoddy material . . . well it would all just get blown away in the first highstorm and leave them sitting on the chamber pot, looking stupid with no walls.

Here, the shanties were confined to smaller road-ways, which stuck out like spokes from this larger one, connecting it to the next large road in line. Many of these were so packed with hanging blankets, people, and improvised houses that you couldn't see the opening on the other side.

Oddly though, it was all up on stilts. Even the most rickety of constructions was up four feet or so in the air. Lift stood at the mouth of one alleyway, hands in pockets, and looked down along the larger slot. As she'd noted earlier, each wall of the city was also a set of shops and homes cut right into the rock, painted to separate them from their neighbors. And for all of them, you had to walk up three or four steps cut into the stone to get in.

"It's like the Purelake," she said. "Everything's up high, like nobody wants to touch the ground 'cuz it's got some kind of nasty cough."

"Wise," Wyndle said. "Protection from the storms."

"The waters should still wash this place away," Lift said.

Well, they obviously didn't, or the place wouldn't be here. She continued strolling down the road, passing lines of homes cut into the wall, and strings of other homes smushed between them. Those shanties looked inviting—warm, packed, full of life. She even saw the green, bobbing motes of lifespren floating along among them, something you usually only saw when there were lots of plants. Unfortunately, she knew from experience that sometimes no matter how inviting a place looked, it wouldn't welcome a foreigner urchin.

"So," Wyndle said, crawling along the wall next to her head, leaving a trail of vines behind him. "You have gotten us here, and—remarkably—avoided incarceration. What now?"

"Food," Lift said, her stomach grumbling.

"You just ate!"

"Yeah. Used up all the energy getting away from the starvin' guards though. I'm hungrier than when I started!"

"Oh, Blessed Mother," he said in exasperation. "Why didn't you simply *wait* in *line* then?"

"Wouldn't have gotten any food that way."

"It doesn't matter, since you burned all the food into Stormlight, then jumped off a wall!"

"But I got to eat pancakes!"

They wove around a group of Tashikki women carrying baskets on their arms, yammering about Liaforan handicrafts. Two unconsciously covered their baskets and gripped the handles tight as Lift passed.

"I can't believe this," Wyndle said. "I *cannot* believe this is my existence. I was a gardener! Respected!

Now, everywhere I go, people look at us as if we're going to pick their pockets."

"Nothing in their pockets," Lift said, looking over her shoulder. "I don't think shiquas even *have* pockets. Those baskets though . . ."

"Did you know we were considering bonding this nice cobbler man instead of you? A very kindly man who took care of children. I could have lived quietly, helping him, making shoes. I could have done an entire *display* of shoes!"

"And the danger that is coming," Lift said. "From the west? If there really *is* a war?"

"Shoes are important to war," Wyndle said, spitting out a splatter of vines on the wall about him—she wasn't sure what that was supposed to mean. "You think the Radiants are going to fight barefoot? We could have made them shoes, that nice old cobbler and me. Wonderful shoes."

"Sounds boring."

He groaned. "You *are* going to slam me into people, aren't you? I'm going to be a weapon."

"What nonsense are you talking about, Voidbringer?"

"I suppose I need to get you to say the Words, don't I? That's my job? Oh, this is *miserable*."

He often said things like this. You probably had to

be messed-up in the brain to be a Voidbringer, so she didn't hold it against him. Instead, she dug in her pocket and brought out a little book. She held it up, flipping through the pages.

"What's that?" Wyndle asked.

"I pinched it from that guard post," she said. "Thought I might be able to sell it or something."

"Let me see that," Wyndle said. He grew down the side of the wall, then up around her leg, twisted around her body, and finally along her arm onto the book. It tickled, the way his main vine shot out tiny creepers that stuck to her skin to keep it in place.

On the page, he spread out other little vines, completely growing over the book and between its pages. "Hmmm..."

Lift leaned back against the wall of the slot as he worked. She didn't feel like she was in a city, she felt like she was in a... tunnel that led to one. Sure, the sky was open and bright overhead, but this street felt so isolated. Usually in a city you could see ripples of buildings, towering off away from you. You could hear shouts from several streets over.

Even clogged with people—more people than seemed reasonable—this street felt isolated. A strange little cremling crawled up the wall beside her. Smaller than most, it was black, with a thin carapace and a strip of fuzzy brown on its back that seemed spongy. Cremlings were strange in Tashikk, and they only got stranger the farther west you went. Closer to the mountains, some of the cremlings could even *fly*.

"Hmm, yes," Wyndle said. "Mistress, this book is likely worthless. It's only a logbook of times the guards have been on duty. The captain, for example, records when she leaves each day—ten on the dot, by the wall clock—replaced by the night watch captain. One visit to the Grand Indicium each week for detailed debriefing of weekly events. She's fastidious, but I doubt anyone will be interested in buying her logbook."

"Surely someone will want it. It's a book!"

"Lift, books have value based on what is *in* them."

"I know. Pages."

"I mean what's on the pages."

"Ink?"

"I mean what the ink *says*."

She scratched her head.

"You really should have listened to those writing coaches in Azir."

"So . . . no trading this for food?" Her stomach growled, attracting more hungerspren.

"Not likely."

Stupid book—and stupid people. She grumbled and tossed the book over her shoulder.

It hit a woman carrying a basket of yarn, unfortunately. She yelped.

"You!" a voice shouted.

Lift winced. A man in a guard's uniform was pointing at her through the crowd.

"Did you just assault that woman?" the guard shouted at her.

"Barely!" Lift shouted back.

The guard came stalking toward her.

"Run?" Wyndle asked.

"Run."

She ducked into an alley, prompting further shouts from the guard, who came barreling in after her.

5

Roughly a half hour later, Lift lay on a stretched-out tarp atop a shanty, puffing from an extended run. That guard had been *persistent.*

She swung idly on the tarp as a wind blew through the shantied alleyway. Beneath, a family talked about the miracle of an entire cart of grain suddenly being dumped in the slums. A mother, three sons, and a father, all together.

I will remember those who have been forgotten. She'd sworn that oath as she'd saved Gawx's life. The right Words, important Words. But what did they mean? What about her mother? Nobody remembered her.

There seemed far too many people out there who were being forgotten. Too many for one girl to re-member.

"Lift?" Wyndle asked. He'd made a little tower of vines and leaves that blew in the wind. "Why haven't you ever gone to the Reshi Isles? That's where you're from, right?"

"It's what Mother said."

"So why not go visit and see? You've been halfway across Roshar and back, to hear you talk. But never to your supposed homeland."

She shrugged, staring up at the late-afternoon sky, feeling the wind. It smelled fresh, compared to the stench of being down in the slots. The city wasn't ripe, but it was thick with contained smells, like animals locked up.

"Do you know why we had to leave Azir?" Lift said softly.

"To chase after that Skybreaker, the one you call Darkness."

"No. We're not doing that."

"Sure."

"We left because people started to know who I am. If you stay in the same place too long, then people start to recognize you. The shopkeepers learn your name. They smile at you when you enter, and already know what to get for you, because they remember what you need."

"That's a bad thing?"

She nodded, still staring at the sky. "It's worse when they think they're your friend. Gawx, the viziers. They make assumptions. They think they know you, then start to expect things of you. Then you have to be the person everyone thinks you are, not the person you actually are."

"And who is the person you actually are, Lift?"

That was the problem, wasn't it? She'd known that once, hadn't she? Or was it just that she'd been young enough not to care?

How did people know? The breeze rocked her perch, and she snuggled up, remembering her mother's arms, her scent, her warm voice.

The pangs of a growling stomach interrupted her, the needs of the now strangling the wants of the past. She sighed and stood up on the tarp. "Come on," she said. "Let's go find some urchins."

6

"Gotta lunks," the little girl said. She was grimy, with hands that probably hadn't been washed since she'd gotten old enough to pick her own nose. She was missing a lot of teeth. Too many for her age. "The marm, she gotta lunks good."

"Gotta lunks for smalls?"

"Gotta lunks for smalls," the girl said to Lift, nodding. "But gotta snaps too. Biga stone, that one, and eyes is swords. Don't lika smalls, but gotta lunks for them. Real nogginin, that."

"Maybe for outsida cares?" Lift said. "Lika the outsida, they gotta light for her, ifn she given lunks for smalls?"

"Maybe," the girl said. "Maybe that right. But it might be nogginin, but it's wrack too. I say that. Real wrack."

"Thanks," Lift said. "Here." She gave the girl her

handkerchief, as promised. In trade for the information.

The girl wrapped it around her head and gave Lift a gap-toothed grin. People liked trading information in Tashikk. It was kind of their thing.

The grimy little girl paused. "That lighta above, the lunks from the sky. I heard loudin about it. That was you, outsida, eh?"

"Yeah."

The girl turned as if to leave, but then reconsidered and put a hand on Lift's arm.

"You," the girl said to Lift. "Outsida?"

"Yeah."

"You listenin'?"

"I'm listenin'."

"People, they don't listen." She smiled at Lift again, then finally scuttled away.

Lift settled back on her haunches in the alleyway across from some communal ovens—a vast, hollowed-out cavern in the wall with huge chimneys cut upward. They burned the rockbud husks from the farms, and anyone could come cook in the central ovens there. They couldn't have fires in their own places. From what Lift had heard, early in the city's life they'd had a fire blaze through the various slums and kill *tons* of people.

In the alleys you didn't see smoke trails, only the

occasional pinprick of spherelight. It was supposed to be the Weeping, and most spheres had gone dun. Only those who had spheres out, by luck, during that unexpected highstorm a few days ago would have light.

"Mistress," Wyndle said, "that was the strangest conversation I've *ever* heard, and I once grew an entire garden for some keenspren."

"Seemed normal to me. Just a kid on the street."

"But the way you talked!" Wyndle said.

"What way?"

"With all those odd words and terms. How did you know what to say?"

"It just felt right," Lift said. "Words is words. Anyway, she said that we could get food at the Tashi's Light Orphanage. Same as the other one we talked to."

"Then why haven't we gone there?" Wyndle asked.

"Nobody likes the woman who runs it. They don't trust her; say that she's starvin' mean. That she only gives away food in the first place because she wants to look good for the officials that watch the place."

"To turn your phrase back at you, mistress, food is food."

"Yeah," Lift said. "It's just . . . what's the challenge of eating a lunch someone *gives* you?"

"I'm certain you will survive the indignity, mistress."

Unfortunately, he was right. She was too hungry

to produce any awesomeness, which meant being a regular child beggar. She didn't move though, not yet.

People, they don't listen. Did Lift listen? She did usually, didn't she? Why did the little urchin girl care, anyway?

Hands in pockets, Lift rose and picked her way through the crowded slot street, dodging the occasional hand that tried to swat or punch her. People here did something strange—they kept their spheres in rows, strung on long strings, even if they put them in pouches. And all the money she saw had holes in the bottoms of the glass spheres, so you could do that. What if you had to count out exact change? Would you unstring the whole starvin' bunch, then string them up again?

At least they used spheres. People farther toward the west, they just used chips of gemstone, sometimes embedded in hunks of glass, sometimes not. Starvin' easy to lose, those were.

People got so mad when she lost spheres. They were strange about money. Far too concerned with something that you couldn't eat—though Lift figured that was probably the point of using spheres instead of something rational, like bags of food. If you actually traded food, everyone would eat up all their money and then where would society be?

The Tashi's Light Orphanage was a corner building, cut into a place where two streets met. The main face pointed onto the large thoroughfare of the immigrant quarter, and was painted bright orange. The other side faced a particularly wide alleyway mouth that had some rows of seats cut into the sides, making a half circle, like some kind of theater—though it was broken in the center for the alleyway. That strung out into the distance, but it didn't look quite as derelict as some others. Some of the shanties even had doors, and the belching that echoed from within the alley sounded almost refined.

She'd been told by the urchins not to approach from the street side, which was for officials and real people. Urchins were to approach from the alleyway side, so Lift neared the stone benches of the little amphitheater—where some old people in shiquas were sitting—and knocked on the door. A section of the stone above it was carved and painted gold and red, though she couldn't read the letters.

A youth pulled open the door. He had a flat, wide face, like Lift had learned to associate with people who weren't born quite the same as other folk. He looked her over, then pointed at the benches. "Sit there," he said. "Food comes later."

"How much later?" Lift said, hands on hips.

"Why? You got *appointments*?" the young man asked, then smiled. "Sit there. Food comes later."

She sighed, but settled down near where the old people were chatting. She got the impression that they were people from farther in the slum who came out here, to the open circle cut into the mouth of the alleyway, where there were steps to sit on and a breeze.

With the sun getting closer to setting, the slots were falling deeper and deeper into shadow. There wouldn't be many spheres to light it up at night; people would probably go to bed earlier than they normally did, as was common during the Weeping. Lift huddled on one of the seats, Wyndle writhing up beside her. She stared at the stupid door to the stupid orphanage, her stupid stomach growling.

"What was wrong with that young man who answered the door?" Wyndle asked.

"Dunno," Lift said. "Some people are just born like that."

She waited on the steps, listening to some Tashikki men from the slums chat and chuckle together. Eventually a figure skulked into the mouth of the alleyway—it seemed to be a woman, wrapped all in dark cloth. Not a true shiqua. Maybe a foreigner trying to wear one, and hide who she was.

The woman sniffled audibly, holding the hand of a

large child, maybe ten or eleven years old. She led him to the doorstep of the orphanage, then pulled him into a hug.

The boy stared ahead, sightless, drooling. He had a scar on his head, healed mostly, but still an angry red.

The woman bowed her head, then her back, and slunk away, leaving the boy. He just sat there, staring. Not a baby in a basket; no, that was a children's tale. This was what actually happened at orphanages, in Lift's experience. People left children who were too big to keep caring for, but couldn't take care of themselves or contribute to the family.

"Did she . . . just leave that boy?" Wyndle asked, horrified.

"She's probably got other children," Lift said softly, "she can barely keep fed. She can't spend all her time looking after one like that, not any longer." Lift's heart twisted inside her and she wanted to look away, but couldn't.

Instead, she stood up and walked over toward the boy. Rich people, like the viziers in Azir, had a strange perspective on orphanages. They imagined them full of saintly little children, plucky and good-hearted, eager to work and have a family.

In Lift's experience though, orphanages had far more like this boy. Kids who were tough to care for.

Kids who required constant supervision, or who were confused in the head. Or those who could get violent.

She hated how rich people made up this romantic dream of what an orphanage should be like. Perfect, full of sweet smiles and happy singing. Not full of frustration, pain, and confusion.

She sat down next to the boy. She was smaller than he was. "Hey," she said.

He looked to her with glazed eyes. She could see his wound better now. The hair hadn't grown back on the side of his head.

"It's going to be all right," she said, taking his hand in hers.

He didn't reply.

A short time later, the door into the orphanage opened, revealing a shriveled-up weed of a woman. Seriously. She looked like the child of a broom and a particularly determined clump of moss. Her skin drooped off her bones like something you'd hack up after catching crud in the slums, and she had spindly fingers that Lift figured might be twigs she'd glued in place after her real ones fell off.

The woman put hands on hips—amazingly, she didn't break any bones in the motion—and looked the two of them over. "An idiot and an opportunist," she said.

"Hey!" Lift said, scrambling up. "He's not an idiot. He's just hurt."

"I was describing you, child," the woman said, then knelt beside the boy with the hurt head. She clicked her tongue. "Worthless, worthless," she muttered. "I can see through your deception. You won't last long here. Watch and see." She gestured backward, and the young man Lift had seen earlier came out and took the hurt boy by the arm, leading him into the orphanage.

Lift tried to follow, but twigs-for-hands stepped in front of her. "You can have three meals," the woman told her. "You pick when you want them, but after three you're done. Consider yourself lucky I'm willing to give anything to one like you."

"What's that supposed to mean?" Lift demanded.

"That if you don't want rats on your ship, you shouldn't be in the business of feeding them." The woman shook her head, then moved to pull the door shut.

"Wait!" Lift said. "I need somewhere to sleep."

"Then you came to the right place."

"Really?"

"Yes, those benches usually clear out once it gets dark."

"Stone *benches*?" Lift said. "You want me to sleep on stone benches?"

"Oh, don't whine. It's not even raining any longer." The woman shut the door.

Lift sighed, looking toward Wyndle. A moment later, the young man from before opened the door and tossed something out to her—a large baked roll of clemabread, thick and granular, with spicy paste at the center.

"Don't suppose you have a pancake?" Lift asked him. "I've got a goal to eat—"

He shut the door. Lift sighed, but settled down on the stone benches near some old men, and started gobbling it up. It wasn't particularly good, but it was warm and filling. "Storming witch," she muttered.

"Don't judge her too harshly, child," said one of the old men on the benches. He wore a black shiqua, but had pulled back the part that wrapped the face, exposing a grey mustache and eyebrows. He had dark brown skin with a wide smile. "It is difficult to be the one that handles everyone else's problems."

"She doesn't have to be so mean."

"When she isn't, then children congregate here begging for handouts."

"So? Isn't that kind of the *point* of an orphanage?" Lift chewed on the roll. "Sleep on the rock benches? I should go steal her pillow."

"I think you'd find her ready to deal with feisty urchin thieves."

"She ain't never faced *me* before. I'm *awesome.*" She looked down at the rest of her food. Of course, if she used her awesomeness, she'd just end up hungry again.

The man laughed. "They call her the Stump, because she won't be blown by any storm. I don't think you'll get the best of her, little one." He leaned in. "But I have information, if you are interested in a trade."

Tashikki and their secrets. Lift rolled her eyes. "Ain't got nothing left to trade."

"Trade me your time, then. I will tell you how to get on the Stump's good side. Maybe earn yourself a bed. In turn, you answer a question for me. Is this a deal?"

Lift cocked an eyebrow at him. "Sure. Whatever."

"Here is my secret. The Stump has a little . . . hobby. She is in the business of trading spheres. An exchanging business, so to speak. Find someone who wants to trade with her, and she will handsomely reward you."

"Trade spheres?" Lift said. "Money for money? What is the point of that?"

He shrugged. "She works hard to cover it up. So it must be important."

"What a lame secret," Lift said. She popped the last of the roll into her mouth, the clemabread breaking apart easily—it was almost more of a mush.

"Will you still answer my question?"

"Depends on how lame *it* is."

"What body part do you feel that you are most like?" he asked. "Are you the hand, always busy doing work? Are you the mind, giving direction? Do you feel that you are more of a . . . leg, perhaps? Bearing up everyone else, and rarely noticed?"

"Yeah. Lame question."

"No, no. It is of most importance. Each person, they are but a piece of something larger—some grand organism that makes up this city. This is the philosophy I am building, you see."

Lift eyed him. Great. Angry twig running an orphanage; weird old man outside it. She dusted off her hands. "If I'm anything, I'm a nose. 'Cuz I'm filled with all kinds of weird crud, and you never know what's gonna fall out."

"Ah . . . interesting."

"That wasn't meant to be helpful."

"Yes, but it was honest, which is the cornerstone of a good philosophy."

"Yeah. Sure." Lift hopped off the stone benches. "As fun as it was talkin' crazy stuff with you, I got somewhere important to be."

"You do?" Wyndle asked, rising from where he'd been coiled up on the bench beside her.

"Yup," Lift said. "I've got an *appointment*."

7

Lift was worried she'd be late. She'd never been good with time.

Now, she could keep the important parts straight. Sun up, sun down. Blah blah. But the divisions beyond that . . . well, she'd never found those to be important. Other people did though, so she hurried through the slot.

"Are you going to find spheres for that woman at the orphanage?" Wyndle said, zipping along the ground beside her, weaving between the legs of people. "Get on her good side?"

"Of course not," Lift said, sniffing. "It's a scam."

"It is?"

"Course it is. She's probably launderin' spheres for criminals, takin' them as 'donations,' then givin' others back. Men'll pay well to clean up their spheres, particularly in places like this, where you got scribes looking over your shoulder all the starvin' time. Course, it might not be *that* scam. She might be guiltin' people into giving her donations of infused spheres, traded for her dun ones. They'll feel sympathetic, because she talks about her poor children. Then she can trade infused spheres to the moneychangers and make a small profit."

"That's *shockingly* unscrupulous, mistress!"

Lift shrugged. "What *else* are you going to do with orphans? Gotta be good for something, right?"

"But profiting off people's emotions?"

"Pity can be a powerful tool. Anytime you can make someone else feel something, you've got power over them."

"I . . . guess?"

"Gotta make sure that never happens to me," Lift said. "It's how you stay strong, see."

She found her way back to the place where she'd entered the slots, then from there poked around until she found the ramp up to the entrance of the city. It was long and shallow, for driving wagons down, if you needed to.

She crawled up it a ways, just enough to get a glimpse at the guard post. There was still a line up there, grown longer than when she'd been in it. Many people were actually making camp on the stones. Some enterprising merchants were selling them food, clean water, and even tents.

Good luck, Lift thought. Most of the people in that line looked like they didn't own much besides their own skins, maybe an exotic disease or two. Lift retreated. She wasn't awesome enough to risk another encounter with the guards. Instead she settled down in a small cleft in the rock at the bottom of the ramp, where she watched a blanket merchant pass. He was using a strange little horse—it was shaggy and white, and had horns on its head. Looked like those animals that were terrible to eat out west.

"Mistress," Wyndle said from the stone wall beside her head, "I don't know much about humans, but I do know a bit about plants. You're remarkably similar. You need light, water, and nourishment. And plants have roots. To anchor them, you see, during storms. Otherwise they blow away."

"It's nice to blow away sometimes."

"And when the great storm comes?"

Lift's eyes drifted toward the west. Toward . . . whatever was building there. *A storm that blows the wrong way,* the viziers had said. *It can't be possible. What game are the Alethi playing?*

A few minutes later, the guard captain walked down the ramp. The woman practically dragged her feet, and as soon as she was out of sight of the guard post, she let her shoulders slump. Looked like it had been a rough day. What could have caused that?

Lift huddled down, but the woman didn't so much as look at her. Once the captain passed, Lift climbed to her feet and scuttled after.

Tailing someone through this town proved easy. There weren't nearly as many hidden nooks or branching paths. As Lift had guessed, now that it was getting dark, the streets were clearing. Maybe there would be an upswing in activity once the first moon got high enough, but for now there wasn't enough light.

"Mistress," Wyndle said. "What are we doing?"

"Just thought I'd see where that woman lives."

"But why?"

Unsurprisingly, the captain didn't live too far from her guard post. A few streets inward, likely far enough to be outside the immigrant quarter but close enough for the place to be cheaper by association. It was a large set of rooms carved into the rock wall, marked by a window for each one. Apartments, rather than one single "building." It did look pretty strange—a sheer rock face, broken by a bunch of shutters.

The captain entered, but Lift didn't follow. Instead, she craned her neck upward. Eventually one of the windows near the top shone with spherelight, and the captain pushed open the shutters for some fresh air.

"Hm," Lift said, squinting in the darkness. "Let's head up that wall, Voidbringer."

"Mistress, you could call me by my name."

"I could call you lotsa stuff," Lift said. "Be glad I don't got much of an imagination. Let's go."

Wyndle sighed, but curved up the outside of the captain's tenement. Lift climbed, using his vines as foot- and handholds. This took her up past a number of windows, but only a few of them were lit. One pair of windows on the same side helpfully had a washing line draped between them, and Lift snatched a shiqua. Nice of them to leave it out, up high enough that only she could get to it.

She didn't stop at the captain's window, which Wyndle seemed to find surprising. She went all the way up to the top and eventually climbed out onto a field of treb, a grain that grew in bunches inside hard pods on vines. The farmers here grew them in little slits in the stone, just under a foot wide. The vines would bunch up in there, and grow pods that got wedged so they didn't tumble free in storms.

The farmers were done for the day, leaving piles of weeds to get carried away in the next storm— whenever that came. Lift settled down on the lip of the trench, looking out over the city. It was pinpricked by spheres. Not many, but more than she'd have expected. That made illumination shine up from the slots, like they were cracks in something bright at the center. How must it look when people had more in-fused spheres? She imagined bright columns of light shining up from the holes.

Below, the captain closed her window and apparently hooded her spheres. Lift yawned. "You don't need sleep, right, Voidbringer?"

"I do not."

"Then keep an eye on that building. Wake me up anytime someone goes into it, or if that captain comes out."

"Could you at least tell me *why* we're spying on a captain of the city watch?"

"What else are we going to do?"

"Anything else?"

"Boring," Lift said, then yawned again. "Wake me up, okay?"

He said something, likely a complaint, but she was already drifting off.

It seemed like only moments before he nudged her awake.

"Mistress?" he said. "Mistress, I find myself in awe of your ingenuity, and your stupidity, both at once."

She yawned, shifting on her stolen shiqua blanket and swatting at some lifespren that were floating around. She hadn't dreamed, thankfully. She hated dreams. They either showed her a life she couldn't have, or a life that terrified her. What was the good of either one?

"Mistress?" Wyndle asked.

She stirred, sitting up. She hadn't realized that she'd picked a spot surrounded by and overgrown with vines, and they'd gotten stuck in her clothing. What was she doing up here again? She ran her hand through her hair, which was snarled and sticking out in all sorts of directions.

Sunlight was peeking up over the horizon, and farmers were already out working again. In fact, now that she'd sat up out of the nest of vines, a few had turned to regard her with baffled looks. It probably wasn't often you found a little Reshi girl sleeping by a cliff in your field. She grinned and waved at them.

"Mistress," Wyndle said. "You told me to warn you if someone went into the building."

Right. She started, remembering what she'd been doing, the fog leaving her mind. "And?" she asked, urgent.

"And Darkness himself, the man who almost killed you in the royal palace, just entered the building below us."

Darkness himself. Lift felt a spike of alarm and gripped the edge of the cliff, barely daring to peek over. She'd wondered if he would come.

"You *did* come to the city chasing him," Wyndle said.

"Pure coincidence," she mumbled.

"No it's not. You showed off your powers to that guard captain, *knowing* that she'd write a report about what she saw. And you knew that would draw Darkness's attention."

"I can't search a whole city for one man; I needed a way to get him to come to me. Didn't expect him to find this place so quickly though. Must have some scribe watching reports."

"But *why*?" Wyndle said, his voice almost a whine. "Why are you looking for him? He's dangerous."

"Obviously."

"Oh, mistress. It's crazy. He—"

"He kills people," she said softly. "The viziers have tracked him. He murders people that don't seem to be connected. The viziers are confused, but I'm not." She took a deep breath. "He's hunting someone in this city, Wyndle. Someone with powers . . . someone like me."

Wyndle trailed off, then slowly let out an "aaahh" of understanding.

"Let's get down to her window," Lift said, ignoring the farmers and climbing over the cliff's edge. It was still dark in the city, which was waking up slowly.

She shouldn't be too conspicuous until things got busier.

Wyndle helpfully grew down in front of her, giving her something to cling to. She wasn't completely sure what drove her. Maybe it was the lure of finding someone else like her, someone who could explain what she was and why her life made no sense these days. Or maybe she just didn't like the idea of Darkness stalking someone innocent. Somebody who, like her, hadn't done anything wrong—well, nothing big— except for having powers he thought they shouldn't.

She pressed her ear against the shutters of the captain's room. Within, she distinctly heard *his* voice.

"A young woman," Darkness said. "Herdazian or Reshi."

"Yes, sir," the captain said. "Do you mind? Can I see your papers again?"

"You will find them in order."

"I just . . . special operative of the prince? I've never heard of the title before."

"It is an ancient but rarely used designation," Darkness said. "Explain exactly what this child did."

"I—"

"Explain again. To me."

"Well, she gave us quite the runaround, sir. Slipped into our guard post, knocked over our things, stole some food. The big crime was when she dumped that grain into the city. I'm sure she did it on purpose; the merchant has already filed suit against the city guard for willful neglect of duty."

"His case is weak," Darkness said. "Because he hadn't yet been approved for admittance into the city, he didn't come under your jurisdiction. If anything he needs to file against the highway guard, and classify it as banditry."

"That's what I told him!"

"You are not to be blamed, Captain. You faced a force you cannot understand, and which I am not at liberty to explain. I need details, however, as proof. Did she glow?"

"I ... well ..."

"Did she *glow*, Captain."

"Yes. I swear, I am of sound mind. I wasn't simply seeing things, sir. She glowed. And the grain glowed too, faintly."

"And she was slippery to the touch?"

"Slicker than if she had been oiled, sir. I've never felt anything like it."

"As anticipated. Here, sign this."

They made some shuffling noises. Lift clung there, ear to the wall, heart pounding. Darkness had a Shardblade. If he suspected she was out here, he could stab through the wall and cut her clean in half.

"Sir?" the guard captain said. "Could you tell me

what's going on here? I feel lost, like a soldier on a battlefield who can't remember which banner is hers."

"It is not material for you to know."

"Um . . . yes, sir."

"Watch for the child. Have others do the same, and report to your superiors if she is discovered. I will hear of it."

"Yes, sir."

Footsteps marked him walking for the door. Before he left, he noted something. "Infused spheres, Captain? You are lucky to have them, these days."

"I traded for them, sir."

"And dun ones in the lantern on the wall."

"They ran out weeks ago, sir. I haven't replaced them. Is this . . . relevant, sir?"

"No. Remember your orders, Captain." He bade her farewell.

The door shut. Lift scrambled up the wall again—trailed by a whimpering Wyndle—and hid there on the top, watching as Darkness stepped out onto the street below. Morning sunlight warmed the back of her neck, and she couldn't keep herself from trembling.

A black and silver uniform. Dark skin, like he was Makabaki, with a pale patch on one cheek: a birthmark shaped like a crescent.

Dead eyes. Eyes that didn't care if they were looking at a man, a chull, or a stone. He tucked some papers into his coat pocket, then pulled on his long-cuffed gloves.

"So we've found him," Wyndle whispered. "Now what?"

"Now?" Lift swallowed. "Now we follow him."

8

Tailing Darkness was a far different experience from tailing the captain. For one, it was daylight now. Still early morning, but light enough that Lift had to worry about being spotted. Fortunately, encountering Darkness had completely burned away the fog of sleepiness she'd felt upon awaking.

At first she tried to stay on the tops of the walls, in the gardens above the city. That proved difficult. Though there were some bridges up here crossing over the slots, they weren't nearly as common as she needed. Each time Darkness hit an intersection she had a shiver of fear, worrying he'd turn down a path she couldn't follow without somehow leaping over a huge gap.

Eventually she took the more dangerous route of scrambling down a ladder, then chasing after him within a trench. Fortunately, it seemed that people in here expected some measure of jostling as they moved through the streets. The confines weren't completely cramped—many of the larger streets had plenty of space. But those walls did enhance the feeling of being boxed in.

Lift had lots of practice with this sort of thing, and she kept the tail inconspicuous. She didn't pick any pockets, despite several fine opportunities—people who were practically holding their pouches up, demanding them to be taken. If she hadn't been following Darkness, she might have grabbed a few for old times' sake.

She didn't use her awesomeness, which was running out anyway. She hadn't eaten since last night, and if she didn't use the power, it eventually vanished. Took about half a day; she didn't know why.

She dodged around the figures of farmers heading to work, women carrying water, kids skipping to their lessons—where they'd sit in rows and listen to a teacher while doing some menial task, like sewing, to pay for the education. Suckers.

People gave Darkness lots of space, moving away from him like they would a guy whose backside couldn't help but let everyone know what he'd been eating lately. She smiled at the thought, climbing along the top of some boxes beside a few other urchins. Darkness, though, he wasn't that *normal*. She had trouble imagining him eating, or anything like that.

A shopkeeper chased them down off the boxes, but Lift had gotten a good look at Darkness and was able to scurry after him, Wyndle at her side.

Darkness never paused to consider his route, or to look at the wares of street vendors. He seemed to move too quickly for his own steps, like he was melting from shadow to shadow as he strode. She nearly lost sight of him several times, which was bizarre. She'd always been able to keep track of where people were.

Darkness eventually reached a market where they sure had a lot of fruit on display. Looked like someone had planned a really, really big food fight, but had decided to call it off and were reluctantly selling their ammunition. Lift helped herself to a purple fruit—she didn't know the name—while the shopkeeper was staring, uncomfortably, at Darkness. As people did. It—

"Hey!" the shopkeeper shouted. "Hey, stop!"

Lift spun, tucking her hand behind her back and dropping the fruit—which she kicked with her heel into the crowd. She smiled sweetly.

But the shopkeeper wasn't looking at her. He was looking at a different opportunist, a girl a few years Lift's senior, who had swiped a whole basket of fruit.

The young woman bolted the moment she was spotted, leaning down and clinging to the basket. She sprinted deftly through the crowd.

Lift heard herself whimper.

No. Not that way. Not toward—

Darkness snatched the young woman from the crowd. He flowed toward her almost as if he were liquid, then seized her by the shoulder with the speed of a snapping rat trap. She struggled, battering against him, though he remained stiff and didn't seem to notice or mind the attack. Still holding to her, he bent and picked up the basket of fruit, then carried it toward the shop, dragging the thief after him.

"Thank you!" the shopkeeper said, taking back the basket and looking over Darkness's uniform. "Um, officer?"

"I am a special deputized operative, granted free jurisdiction throughout the kingdom by the prince," Darkness said, removing a sheet of paper from his coat pocket and holding it up.

The girl grabbed a piece of fruit from the basket and threw it at Darkness, bouncing it off his chest with a splat. He didn't respond to this, and didn't even flinch as she bit his hand. He just tucked away the document he'd been showing the shopkeeper. Then he looked at her.

Lift knew what it was like to meet those cold, glassy

eyes. The girl in his grip cringed before him, then seemed to panic, reaching to her belt, yanking out her knife and brandishing it. She tried a desperate swing at Darkness's arm, but he easily slapped the weapon away with his empty hand.

Around them, the crowd had sensed that something was off. Though the rest of the market was busy, this one section grew still. Lift pulled back beside a small, broken cart—built narrow for navigating the slots—where several other urchins were betting on how long it would be before Tiqqa escaped "this time."

As if in response to this, Darkness summoned his Shardblade and rammed it through the struggling girl's chest.

The long blade sank up to its hilt as he pulled her onto it, and she gasped, eyes going wide—then shriveling and burning out, letting twin trails of smoke creep toward the sky.

The shopkeeper screamed, hand to his chest. He dropped the basket of fruit.

Lift squeezed her eyes closed. She heard the corpse drop to the ground, and Darkness's too-calm voice as he said, "Give this form to the market watch, who will dispose of the body and take your statement. Let me witness the time and date . . . here. . . ."

Lift forced her eyes open. The two urchins beside her gaped in horror, mouths wide. One started crying with a disbelieving whine.

Darkness finished filling out the form, then prodded the shopkeeper, forcing the man to witness it as well in pen, and write a short description of what had happened.

That done, Darkness nodded and turned to go. The shopkeeper—fruit spilled at his feet, a stack of boxes and baskets to his side—stared at the corpse, papers held limply in his fingers. Then angerspren boiled up around him, like red pools on the ground.

"Was that *necessary*!" he demanded. "Tashi ... Tashi above!"

"Tashi doesn't care much for what you do here," Darkness said as he walked away. "In fact, I'd pray that he doesn't reach your city, as I doubt you'd like the consequences. As for the thief, she would have enjoyed imprisonment for her theft. The punishment prescribed for assaulting an officer with a bladed weapon, however, is death."

"But ... *But that was barbaric!* Couldn't you have just ... taken off her hand or ... or ... something?"

Darkness stopped, then looked back at the shopkeeper, who cringed.

"I have tried that, where the law allows discretion

in punishments," Darkness said. "Removing a hand leads to a high rate of recidivism, as the thief is left unable to do most honest work, and therefore must steal. In such a case, I could make crime worse instead of reducing it."

He cocked his head, looking from the shopkeeper to the corpse, as if confused why anyone would be bothered by what he had done. Without further concern for the matter, he turned and continued on his way.

Lift stared, stunned, then—heedless of being seen—forced away her shock and ran to the fallen girl. She grabbed the body by the shoulders and leaned down, breathing out her awesomeness—the light that burned inside her—and imparting it to the dead young woman.

For a moment it seemed to be working. She saw something, a luminescence in the shape of a figure. It vibrated around the corpse, quivering. Then it puffed away, and the body remained on the ground, immobile, eyes burned.

"No . . ." Lift said.

"Too much time passed for this one, mistress," Wyndle said softly. "I'm sorry."

"Gawx was longer."

"Gawx wasn't slain by a Shardblade," Wyndle said.

"I . . . I think that humans don't die instantly, most of the time. Oh, my memory. Too many holes, mistress. But I do know that a Shardblade, it is different. Maybe if you'd reached this one right after. Yes, you'd have been able to then. It was just too long. And you don't have enough power, either way."

Lift knelt on the stones, drained. The body didn't even bleed.

"She *did* draw a knife on him," Wyndle said, his voice small.

"She was terrified! She saw his eyes and panicked." She gritted her teeth, then snarled and climbed to her feet. She scrambled over to the shopkeeper, who jumped back as Lift seized two of his fruits and stared him right in the eyes as she took a big, juicy bite of one and chewed.

Then she chased after Darkness.

"Mistress . . ." Wyndle said.

She ignored him. She followed after the heartless creature, the murderer. She managed to find him again—he left an even bigger wake of disturbed people behind him now. She caught sight of him as he left the market, going up a set of steps, then walking through a large archway.

Lift followed carefully, and peeked out into an odd section of the city. They'd carved a large, conical chunk out of the stone here. It was deep a ways, and was filled with water.

It was a really, really big cistern. A cistern as big as several houses, to collect rain from the storms.

"Ah," Wyndle said. "Yes, separated from the rest of the city by a raised rim. Rainwater in the streets will flow outward, rather than toward this cistern, keeping it pure. In fact, it seems that most of the streets have a slope to them, to siphon water outward. Where does it go from there though?"

Whatever. She inspected the big cistern, which did have a neat bridge running across it. The thing was so big that you needed a bridge, and people stood on it to lower buckets on ropes down into the water.

Darkness didn't take the path across the bridge; there was a ledge running around the outside of the cistern also, and there were fewer people on it. He obviously wanted to take the route that involved less jostling.

Lift hesitated at the entrance into the place, fighting with her frustration, her sense of powerlessness. She earned a curse or two as she accidentally blocked traffic.

Her name was Tiqqa, Lift thought. *I will remember you, Tiqqa. Because few others will.*

Below, the large cistern pool rippled from the many people drawing water from it. If she followed Darkness around the ledge, she'd be in the open with nobody between them.

Well, he didn't look behind himself very often. She just had to risk it. She took a step along the path.

"Don't!" Wyndle said. "Mistress, stay hidden. He has eyes you cannot see."

Fine. She joined the flow of people moving down the steps. This was the shorter route, but there were a *lot* of people on the bridge. In the bustle, because of her shortness, she lost sight of Darkness.

Sweat prickled on the back of her neck, cold. If she couldn't see him, she felt certain—irrationally—that he was now watching her. She pictured again and again how he'd emerged from the market to grab the thief, a supernatural ease to his movements. Yes, he knew things about people like Lift. He'd spoken of her powers with familiarity.

Lift drew upon her awesomeness. She didn't make herself Slick, but she let the light suffuse her, pep her up. The power felt like it was alive sometimes. The essence of eagerness, a spren. It drove her forward as she dodged and squeezed through the crowd of people on the bridge.

She reached the other side of the bridge, and saw no sign of Darkness on the ledge. Storms. She left through the archway on the other side, slipping back into the city proper and entering a large crossroads.

Shiqua-wrapped Tashikkis passed in front of her, interrupted occasionally by Azish in colorful patterns. This was certainly a better part of town. Light from the rising sun sparkled off painted sections of the walls, here displaying a grand mural of Tashi and the Nine binding the world. Some of the people she passed had parshman slaves, their marbled skin black and red. She hadn't seen many of those here, not as many as in Azir. Maybe she just hadn't been in rich enough sections of the city.

Lots of the buildings here had small trees or ornamental shrubs in front of them. They were bred and cultivated to be lazy, so their leaves didn't pull in despite the near crowds.

Read those crowds . . . Lift thought. *The people. Where are the people being strange?*

She scrambled through the crossroads, intuiting the way. Something about how people stood, where they looked. There was a ripple here. The waves of a passing fish, silent but not still.

She turned a corner, and caught a brief glimpse of Darkness striding up a set of stairs beside a row of small trees. He stepped into a building, then shut the door.

Lift crept up beside the building Darkness had entered, her face brushing the leaves of the trees, causing them to pull in. They were lazy, but not so stupid that they wouldn't move if touched.

"What are these 'eyes' you say he has?" she asked as Wyndle wound up beside her. "The ones I can't see."

"He will have a spren," Wyndle said. "Like me. It's likely invisible to you and anyone else but him. Most are, on this side, I think. I don't remember all the rules."

"You sure are dumb some of the time, Voidbringer."

He sighed.

"Don't worry," Lift said. "I'm dumb *most* of the time." She scratched her head. The steps ended at a door. Did she dare open it and slip in? If she was going to learn anything about Darkness and what he was doing in the city, she'd have to do more than find out where he lived.

"Mistress," Wyndle said, "I might be stupid, but I can say with certainty that you're *not* a match for that creature. There are many Words you haven't spoken."

"Course I haven't said those kinds of words," Lift said. "Don't you ever listen to me? I'm a sweet, innocent little girl. I ain't going to talk about bollocks and jiggers and stuff. I'm not *crass*."

Wyndle sighed. "Not *those* kinds of words. Mistress, I—"

"Oh, hush," Lift said, squatting beside the trees lining the front of the building. "We have to get in there and see what he's up to."

"Mistress, please don't get yourself killed. It would

be *traumatic.* Why, I think it would take me months and months to get over it!"

"That's faster than I'd get over it." She scratched at her head. She couldn't hang on the side of the building and listen at Darkness, like she had at the guard captain's place. Not in a fancy part of town, and not in the middle of the day.

Besides, she had loftier goals today than just eavesdropping. She had to actually break into this place to do what she needed to do here. But how? It wasn't like these buildings had back doors. They were cut directly into the rock. She could maybe get in one of the front windows, but that sure would be suspicious.

She glanced at the passing crowds. People in cities, they'd notice something like an urchin breaking in through a window. Something that looked like trouble. But other times they'd ignore the most obvious things in front of their own noses.

Maybe . . . She did have awesomeness left from that fruit she'd eaten. She eyed a shuttered window about five or six feet up. That would be on the first story of the building, but it was up somewhat high, because everything was built up a ways in this city.

Lift hunkered down and let some of her awesomeness out. The little tree beside her stretched and popped softly. Leaves budded, unfurled, and gave a good-morning yawn. Branches reached toward the sky. Lift took her time, filling in the tree's canopy, letting it get large enough to obscure the window. Around her feet, seeds from storm-blown rockbuds puffed up like little hot buns. Vines wrapped around her ankles.

Nobody passing on the street noticed. They'd cuff an urchin for scratching her butt in a suspicious manner, but couldn't be bothered with a miracle. Lift sighed, smiling. The tree would cover her as she broke in through that window, if she moved carefully. She let her awesomeness continue to trickle out, comforting the tree, making it even more lazy. Lifespren popped up, little glowing green motes that bobbed around her.

She waited for a lull in the passing crowds, then hopped up and grabbed a branch, hauling herself into the tree. The tree, drinking of her awesomeness, didn't pull its leaves back in. She felt safe here surrounded by the branches, which smelled rich and heady, like the spices used for broth. Vines wrapped around the tree branches, sprouting leaves, much as Wyndle did.

Unfortunately, her power was almost out. A couple pieces of fruit didn't provide much. She pressed her ear against the window's thick stormshutters, and didn't hear anything from the room beyond. Safe in the tree, she softly rattled the stormshutters with her palms, using the sound to pick out where the latch was.

See. I can listen.

But of course, this wasn't the right kind of listening.

The window was latched with some kind of long bar on the other side, probably fitted into slots across the back of the shutters. Fortunately, these stormshutters weren't as tight as those in other towns; they probably didn't need to be, down here safe in the trenches. She let the vines wind around the branches, drinking of her Stormlight, then twist around her arms and squeeze through cracks in the shutters. The vines stretched up the inside of the shutters, pressing up the bar that held the shutters closed, and . . .

And she was in. She used the last of her awesomeness to coat the hinges of the shutters, so they slid against one another without a hint of a sound. She slipped into a boxlike stone room, lifespren pouring in behind her, dancing in the air like glowing whispermill seeds.

"Mistress!" Wyndle said, growing in onto the wall. "Oh, mistress. That was *delightful*! Why don't we forget this entire mess with the Skybreakers, and go . . . why . . . why, go *run a farm*! Yes, a farm. A lovely farm. You could sculpt plants every day, and eat until you were ready to burst! And . . . Mistress?"

Lift padded through the room, noting a rack of

swords by the wall, sheathed and deadly. Sparring leathers on the floor near the corner. The smell of oil and sweat. There was no door in the doorway, and she peeked out into a dark hallway, listening.

There was a three-way intersection here. Hallways lined with rooms led to her left and right, and then a longer hallway led straight forward, into darkness. Voices echoed from that direction.

That hallway in front of her cut deeper into the stone, away from windows—and from exits. She glanced right instead, toward the building's entrance. An old man sat in a chair there, near the door, wearing a white and black uniform of the type she'd only seen on Darkness and his men. He was mostly bald, except for a few wisps of hair, and had beady eyes and a pinched face—like a shriveled-up fruit that was trying to pass for human.

He stood up and checked a little window in the door, watching the crowd outside with suspicion. Lift took the opportunity to scuttle into the hallway to her left, where she ducked into the next room over.

This looked more promising. Though it was dim with the stormshutters closed, it seemed like some kind of workroom or den. Lift eased open the shutters for a little light, then did a quick search. Nothing obvious on the shelves full of maps. Nothing on the writing table but some books and a rack of spanreeds.

There was a trunk by the wall, but it was locked. She was beginning to despair when she smelled something.

She peeked out of the doorway. That guard had wandered off; she could hear him whistling somewhere, alongside the sound of a stream of liquid in a chamber pot.

Lift slipped farther down the corridor to her left, away from the guard. The next room in line was a bedroom with a door that was cracked open. She slipped in and found a stiff coat hanging on a peg right inside—one with a circular fruit stain on the front. Darkness's jacket for sure.

Below it, sitting on the floor, was a tray with a metal covering—the type fancy people put over plates so they wouldn't have to look at food while it got cold. Underneath, like the emerald treasures of the Tranquiline Halls, Lift found three plates of pancakes.

Darkness's breakfast. Mission accomplished.

She started stuffing her face with a vengeful enthusiasm.

Wyndle made a face from vines beside her. "Mistress? Was this all . . . was this all so you could *steal his food*?"

"Yeph," Lift said, then swallowed. "Course it is." She took another bite. That'd show him.

"Oh. Of course." He sighed deeply. "I suppose this

is . . . this is pleasant, then. Yes. No swinging about of innocent spren, stabbing them into people and the like. Just . . . just stealing some food."

"*Darkness's* food." She'd stolen from a palace, and the starvin' emperor of Azir. She'd needed *something* interesting to try next.

It felt good to finally get enough food to fill her stomach. One of the pancakes was salty, with chopped-up vegetables. Another tasted sweet. The third variety was fluffier, almost without any substance to it, though there was some kind of sauce to dip it in. She slurped that down—who had time for dipping?

She ate every scrap, then settled back against the wall, smiling.

"So, we came all this way," Wyndle said, "and tracked the most dangerous man we've ever met, merely so you could steal his breakfast. We didn't come here to do . . . to do anything more, then?"

"Do you want to do something more?"

"Storms, no!" Wyndle said. He twisted his little vine face around, looking toward the hallway. "I mean . . . every moment we spend in here is dangerous."

"Yup."

"We should run. Go found a farm, like I said. Leave him behind, though he's likely tracking someone in this city. Someone like us, someone who can't fight him. Someone he will murder before they even start to grasp their powers . . ."

They sat in the room, empty tray beside them. Lift felt her awesomeness begin to stir within her again.

"So," she asked. "Guess we go spy on them, eh?"

Wyndle whimpered, but—shockingly—nodded.

9

"Just try not to die too violently, mistress," Wyndle said as she crept closer to the sounds of people talking. "A nice rap on the head, rather than a disemboweling."

That voice was definitely Darkness. The sound of it gave her chills. When the man had confronted her in the Azish palace, he'd been dispassionate, even as he half apologized for what he was about to do.

"I hear that suffocation is nice," Wyndle said. "Though in such a case, don't look at me as you expire. I'm not sure I could handle it."

Remember the girl in the market. Steady.

Storms, her hands were trembling.

"I'm not sure about falling to your death," Wyndle added. "Seems like it might be messy, but at the same time at least there wouldn't be any *stabbing*."

The hallway ended at a large chamber lit by diamonds

that gave it a calm, easy light. Not chips, not even spheres. Larger, unset gemstones. Lift crouched by the half-open door, hidden in shadows.

Darkness—wearing a stiff white shirt—paced before two underlings in uniforms in black and white, with swords at their waists. One was a Makabaki man with a round, goofish face. The other was a woman with skin a shade lighter—she looked like she might be Reshi, particularly with that long dark hair she kept in a tight braid. She had a square face, strong shoulders, and *way* too small a nose. Like she'd sold hers off to buy some new shoes, and was using one she'd dug out of the trash as a replacement.

"Your excuses do not befit those who would join our order," Darkness was saying. "If you would earn the trust of your spren, and take the step from initiate to Shardbearer, you must dedicate yourselves. You must prove your worth. Earlier today I followed a lead that each of you missed, and have discovered a second offender in the city."

"Sir!" the Reshi woman said. "I prevented an assault in an alleyway! A man was being accosted by thugs!"

"While this is well," Darkness said, still pacing back and forth in a calm, even stroll, "we must be careful not to be distracted by petty crimes. I realize that it can be difficult to remain focused when confronted by a fracture of the codes that bind society. Remember that greater matters, and greater crimes, must be our primary concern."

"Surgebinders," the woman said.

Surgebinders. People like Lift, people with awesomeness, who could do the impossible. She hadn't been afraid to sneak into a palace, but huddled by that door—looking in at the man she had named Darkness—she found herself terrified.

"But . . ." said the male initiate. "Is it really . . . I mean, shouldn't we *want* them to return, so we won't be the only order of Knights Radiant?"

"Unfortunately, no," Darkness said. "I once thought as you, but Ishar made the truth clear to me. If the bonds between men and spren are reignited, then men will naturally discover the greater power of the oaths. Without Honor to regulate this, there is a small chance that what comes next will allow the Voidbringers to again make the jump between worlds. That would cause a Desolation, and even a small chance that the world will be destroyed is a risk that we cannot take. Absolute fidelity to the mission Ishar gave us—the greater law of protecting Roshar—is required."

"You're wrong," a voice whispered from the darkness. "You may be a god . . . but you're still wrong."

Lift nearly jumped clear out of her own skin. Storms! There was a guy sitting just inside the doorway, *right next to where she was hiding.* She hadn't seen him—she'd been too fixated on Darkness.

He sat on the floor, wearing tattered white clothing. His hair was short, a brown fuzz, as if he'd kept it shaved until recently. He had pale, ghostly skin, and held a long sword in a silvery sheath, pommel resting against his shoulder, length stretching alongside his body and legs. He held his arms draped around the sheath, as if it were a child's toy to hug.

He shifted in his place, and . . . storms, he left a soft white *afterimage* behind him, like you get when staring at a bright gemstone for too long. It faded away in a moment.

"They're already back," he whispered, speaking with a smooth, airy Shin accent. "The Voidbringers have already returned."

"You are mistaken," Darkness said. "The Voidbringers are not back. What you saw on the Shattered Plains are simply remnants from millennia ago. Voidbringers who have been hiding among us all this time."

The man in white looked up, and Lift shied away. His movement left another afterimage that glowed briefly before fading. Storms. White clothing. Strange powers. Shin man with a bald head. Shardblade.

This was the starvin' *Assassin in White!*

"I saw them return," the assassin whispered. "The

new storm, the red eyes. You are wrong, Nin-son-God. You are wrong."

"A fluke," Darkness said, his voice firm. "I contacted Ishar, and he assured me it is so. What you saw are a few listeners who remain from the old days, ones free to use the old forms. They summoned a cluster of Voidspren. We've found remnants of them on Roshar before, hiding."

"The storm? The new storm, of red lightning?"

"It means nothing," Darkness said. He did not seem to mind being challenged. He didn't seem to mind anything. His voice was perfectly even. "An oddity, to be sure."

"You're wrong. So wrong . . ."

"The Voidbringers have not returned," Darkness said firmly. "Ishar has promised it, and he will not lie. We must do our duty. You are questioning, Szeth-son-Neturo. This is not good; this is weakness. To question is to accept a descent into inactivity. The only path to sanity and action is to choose a code and to follow it. This is why I came to you in the first place."

Darkness turned, striding past the others. "The minds of men are fragile, their emotions mutable and often unpredictable. The *only* path to Honor is to stick to your chosen code. This was the way of the Knights Radiant, and is the way of the Skybreakers."

The man and woman standing nearby both saluted. The assassin just bowed his head again, closing his eyes, holding to that strange silver-sheathed Shardblade.

"You said that there is a second Surgebinder in the city," the woman said. "We can find—"

"She is mine," Darkness said evenly. "You will continue your mission. Find the one who has been hiding here since we arrived." He narrowed his eyes. "If we don't stop one, others will congregate. They clump together. I have often found them making contact with one another, these last five years, if I leave them alone. They must be drawn to each other."

He turned toward his two initiates; he seemed to ignore the assassin except when spoken to. "Your quarry will make mistakes—they will break the law. The other orders always did consider themselves beyond the reach of the law. Only the Skybreakers ever understood the importance of boundaries. Of picking something external to yourself and using it as a guide. Your minds cannot be trusted. Even my mind—especially my mind—cannot be trusted.

"I have given you enough help. You have my blessing and you have our commission granting us authority to act in this city. You will find the Surgebinder, you will discover their sins, and you will bring them judgment. In the name of all Roshar."

The two saluted again, and the room suddenly darkened. The woman began glowing with a phantom light, and she blushed, looking sheepishly toward Darkness. "I'll find them, sir! I have an investigation in progress."

"I have a lead too," the man said. "I'll have the information by tonight for certain."

"Work together," Darkness said. "This is not a competition. It is a test to measure competence. I'm giving you until sunset, but after that I can wait no longer. Now that others have begun arriving, the risk is too great. At sunset, I will deal with the issue myself."

"Bollocks," Lift whispered. She shook her head, then scuttled back along the hallway, away from the group of people.

"Wait," Wyndle said, following. "Bollocks? I thought you claimed you didn't say words like—"

"They've all got 'em," Lift said. "'Cept the girl, though with that face I can't be certain. Anyway, what I said wasn't crass, 'cuz it was just an *observation*." She hit the intersection of corridors, and peeked to the left. The old man on watch was dozing. That let Lift slip across, into the room where she'd first entered. She climbed out into the tree, then closed the shutters.

In seconds she'd run around a corner into an alleyway, where she let herself slide down until she was sitting with her back against the stone, her heart pounding. Farther into the alleyway here, a family ate pancakes in a somewhat nice shanty. It had two whole walls.

"Mistress?" Wyndle said.

"I'm hungry," she complained.

"You just ate!"

"That was catching me up for spending so much getting into that starvin' building." She squeezed her eyes closed, containing her worry.

Darkness's voice was so cold.

But they're like me. They glow like me. They're ... awesome, like I am? What in Damnation is going on?

And the Assassin in White. Was he going to go off and kill Gawx?

"Mistress?" Wyndle coiled around her leg. "Oh, mistress. Did you hear what they called him? Nin? That's a name of Nalan, the Herald! That can't be true. They went away, didn't they? Even we have legends about that. If that creature is truly one of them ... oh, Lift. What are we going to do?"

"I don't know," she whispered. "I don't know. Storms ... why am I even here?"

"I believe I've been asking that since—"

"Shut it, Voidbringer," she said, forcing herself to roll over and get to her knees. Deeper into the cramped alley, the father of the family reached for a cudgel while the wife tugged the curtain closed on the front of their hovel.

Lift sighed, then went wandering back toward the immigrant quarter.

10

When she arrived at the orphanage, Lift finally figured out why it had been set up next to this open space at the mouth of the alleyway. The orphanage caretaker—the Stump, as she'd been called—had opened the doors and let the children out. They played here, in the most boring playground ever. A set of amphitheater steps and some open floor.

The children seemed to love it. They ran up and down the steps, laughing and giggling. Others sat in circles on the ground, playing games with painted pebbles. Laughterspren—like little silver fish that zipped through the air, this way and that—danced in the air some ten feet up, a whole school of the starvin' things.

There were lots of children, younger on average than Lift had assumed. Most, as she had been able to guess, were the kind that were different in the head, or they were missin' an arm or leg. Things like that.

Lift idled near the wide alleyway mouth, near where two blind girls played a game. One would drop rocks of a variety of sizes and shapes, and the other would try to guess which was which, based on how they sounded when they hit the ground. The group of old men and women in shiquas from the day before had again gathered at the back of the half-moon amphitheater seats, chatting and watching the children play.

"I thought you said orphanages were miserable," Wyndle said, coating the wall beside her.

"Everyone gets happy for a little while when you let them go outside," Lift said, watching the Stump. The wizened old lady was scowling as she pulled a cart through the doors toward the amphitheater. More clemabread rolls. Delightful. Those were only *slightly* better than gruel, which was only *slightly* better than cold socks.

Still, Lift joined the others who got in line to accept their roll. When her turn came, the Stump pointed to a spot beside the cart and didn't speak a word to her. Lift stepped aside, lacking the energy to argue.

The Stump made sure every child got a roll, then studied Lift before handing her one of the last two. "Your second meal of three."

"Second!" Lift snapped. "I ain't—"

"You got one last night."

"I didn't ask for it!"

"You ate it." The Stump pushed the cart away, eating the last of the rolls herself.

"Storming witch," Lift muttered, then found a spot on the stone seats. She sat apart from the regular orphans; she didn't want to be talked at.

"Mistress," Wyndle said, climbing the steps to join her. "I don't believe you when you say you left Azir because they were trying to dress you in fancy clothing and teach you to read."

"Is that so," she said, chewing on her roll.

"You liked the clothing, for one thing. And when they tried to give you lessons, you seemed to enjoy the game of always being gone when they came looking. They weren't forcing you into anything; they were merely offering opportunities. The palace was *not* the stifling experience you imply."

"Maybe not for me," she admitted.

It was for Gawx. They expected all *kinds* of things of the new emperor. Lessons, displays. People came to watch him eat every meal. They even got to watch him sleeping. In Azir, the emperor was owned by the people, like a friendly stray axehound that seven different houses fed, all claiming her as their own.

"Maybe," Lift said, "I just didn't want people expecting so much from me. If you get to know people too long, they'll start depending on you."

"Oh, and you can't bear responsibility?"

"Course I can't. I'm a starvin' street urchin."

"One who came here chasing down what *appears* to be one of the Heralds themselves, gone mad and accompanied by an assassin who has murdered *multiple* world monarchs. Yes, I believe that you *must* be avoiding responsibility."

"You giving me lip, Voidbringer?"

"I think so? Honestly, I don't know what that term means, but judging by your tone, I'd say that I'm probably giving you lip. And you probably deserve it."

She grunted in response, chewing on her food. It tasted terrible, as if it had been left out all night.

"Mama always told me to travel," Lift said. "And go places. While I'm young."

"And that's why you left the palace."

"Dunno. Maybe."

"Utter nonsense. Mistress, what is it really? Lift, what do you *want*?"

She looked down at the half-eaten roll in her hand.

"Everything is changing," she said softly. "That's okay. Stuff changes. It's just that, I'm not supposed to. I *asked* not to. She's supposed to give you what you ask."

"The Nightwatcher?" Wyndle asked.

Lift nodded, feeling small, cold. Children played and laughed all around, and for some reason that only made her feel worse. It was obvious to her, though she'd tried ignoring it for years, that she *was* taller than she'd been when she'd first sought out the Old Magic three years ago.

She looked beyond the kids, toward the street passing out front. A group of women bustled past, carrying baskets of yarn. A prim Alethi man strode in the other direction, with straight black hair and an imperious attitude. He was at least a foot taller than anyone else on the street. Workers moved along, cleaning the street, picking up trash.

In the alleyway mouth, the Stump had deposited her cart and was disciplining a child who had started hitting others. At the back of the amphitheater seats, the old men and women laughed together, one pouring cups of tea to pass around.

They all seemed to just . . . know what to do. Cremlings knew to scuttle, plants knew to grow. Everything had its place.

"The only thing I've ever known how to do was hunt food," Lift whispered.

"What's that, mistress?"

It had been hard, at first. Feeding herself. Over time, she'd figured out the tricks. She'd gotten good at it.

But once you weren't hungry all the time, what did you *do*? How did you *know*?

Someone poked at her arm, and she turned to see

that a kid had scooted up beside her—a lean boy with his head shaved. He pointed at her half-eaten roll and grunted.

She sighed and gave it to him. He ate eagerly.

"I know you," she said, cocking her head. "You're the one whose mother dropped him off last night."

"Mother," he said, then looked at her. "Mother . . . come back when?"

"Huh. So you *can* talk," Lift said. "Didn't think you could, after all that staring around dumbly last night."

"I . . ." The boy blinked, then looked at her. No drooling. Must be a good day for him. A grand accomplishment. "Mother . . . come back?"

"Probably not," Lift said. "Sorry, kid. They don't come back. What's your name?"

"Mik," the boy said. He looked at her, confused, as if searching—and failing—to figure out who she was. "We . . . friends?"

"Nope," Lift said. "You don't wanna be my friend. My friends end up as emperors." She shivered, then leaned in. "People *pick his nose* for him."

Mik looked at her blankly.

"Yeah. I'm serious. They pick his nose. Like, he's got this woman who does his hair, and I peeked in, and I saw her sticking something up his nose. Like little tweezers she used to grab his boogies or something." Lift shivered. "Being an emperor is real strange."

The Stump dragged over one of the kids who'd been fighting and plopped him on the stone. Then, oddly, she gave him some earmuffs—like it was cold or something. He put them on and closed his eyes.

The Stump paused, looking toward Lift and Mik. "Making plans on how to rob me?"

"What?" Lift said. "No!"

"One more meal," the woman said, holding up a finger. Then she stabbed it toward Mik. "And when you go, take that one. I *know* he's faking."

"Faking?" Lift turned toward Mik, who blinked, dazed, as if trying to follow the conversation. "You're not serious."

"I can see through it when urchins are feigning illness in order to get food," the Stump snapped. "That one's no idiot. He's pretending." She stomped away.

Mik wilted, looking down at his feet. "I miss Mother."

"Yeah," Lift said. "Nice, eh?"

Mik looked at her, frowning.

"We get to remember ours," Lift said, standing. "That's more than most like us get." She patted him on the shoulder.

A short time later, the Stump called that playtime was over. She herded the kids into the orphanage for naps, though many were too old for that. The Stump gave Mik a displeased eye as he entered, but let him in.

Lift remained in her seat on the stone, then smacked

her hand at a cremling that had been inching across the step nearby. Starvin' thing dodged, then clicked its chitin legs as if laughing. They sure did have strange cremlings here. Not like the ones she was used to at all. Weird how you could forget you were in a different country until you saw the cremlings.

"Mistress," Wyndle said, "have you decided what we're going to do?"

Decide. Why did she have to decide? She usually just *did* things. She'd taken challenges as they'd arisen, gone places for no reason other than that she hadn't seen them before.

The old people who had been watching the children slowly rose, like ancient trees releasing their branches after a storm. One by one they trailed off until only one remained, wearing a black shiqua with the wrap pulled down to expose a face with a grey mustache.

"Ey," Lift called to him. "You still creepy, old man?"

"I am the man I was made to be," he said back.

Lift grunted, climbing from her spot and strolling over to him. Some of the kids from before had left their pebbles, with painted colors that were rubbing off. A poor kid's imitation of glass marbles. Lift kicked at them.

"How do you know what to do?" she asked the man, her hands shoved in her pockets.

"About what, little one?"

"About *everything*," Lift said. "Who tells you how to decide what to do with your time? Was it your parents who showed you? What's the secret?"

"The secret to what?"

"To being human," Lift said softly.

"That," the man said, chuckling, "I don't think I know. At least not better than you do."

Lift looked at the sky, up along slotlike walls, scraped clean of vegetation but painted a dark green, as if in imitation of it.

"It is strange," the man said. "People get such a small amount of time. So many I've known say it—as soon as you feel you're getting a handle on things, the day is done, the night falls, and the light goes out."

Lift looked at him. Yup. Still creepy. "I guess when you're old and stuff, you get to thinkin' about being dead. Kind of like when a fellow's got to piss, he starts thinkin' about finding a convenient alleyway."

The man chuckled. "Your life may pass, but the organism that is the city will continue on. Little nose."

"I'm *not* a nose," Lift said. "I was being cheeky."

"Nose, cheek. Both are on the face."

Lift rolled her eyes. "That's not what I meant either."

"What are you then? An ear, perhaps?"

"Dunno. Maybe."

"No. Not yet. But close."

"Riiight," Lift said. "And what are you?"

"I change, moment by moment. One moment I am the eyes that inspect so many people in this city. Another moment I am the mouth, to speak the words of philosophy. They spread like a disease—and so at times I *am* the disease. Most diseases live. Did you know that?"

"You're . . . not really talking about what you're talking about, are you?" Lift said.

"I believe that I am."

"Great." Of all the people she'd chosen to ask about how to be a responsible adult, she'd picked the one with vegetable soup in place of brains. She turned to go.

"What will you make for this city, child?" the man asked. "That is part of my question. Do you choose, or are you simply molded by the greater good? And are you, as a city, a district of grand palaces? Or are you a slum, unto yourself?"

"If you could see inside me," Lift said, turning and walking backward so she faced the old man on the steps, "you wouldn't say things like that."

"Because?"

"Because. At least slums know what they was built for." She turned and joined the flow of people on the street.

11

I don't think you understand how this is supposed to work," Wyndle said, curling along the wall beside her. "Mistress, you . . . don't seem interested in evolving our relationship."

She shrugged.

"There are Words," Wyndle said. "That's what we call them, at least. They're more . . . ideas. Living ideas, with power. You have to let them into your soul. Let *me* into your soul. You heard those Skybreakers, right? They're looking to take the next step in their training. That's when . . . you know . . . they get a Shardblade. . . ."

He smiled at her, the expression appearing in successive patterns of his growing vines along the wall as they chased her. Each image of the smile was slightly different, grown one after another beside her, like a hundred paintings. They made a smile, and yet none of them *was* the smile. It was, somehow, all of them together. Or perhaps the smile existed in the spaces between the images in the succession.

"There's only one thing I know how to do," Lift said. "And that's steal Darkness's lunch. Like I came to do in the first place."

"And, um, didn't we do that already?"

"Not his food. His lunch." She narrowed her eyes.

"Ah . . ." Wyndle said. "The person he's planning to execute. We're going to snatch them away from him."

Lift strolled along a side street, and ended up passing into a garden: a bowl-like depression in the stone with four exits down different roads. Vines coated the leeward side of the wall, but they slowly gave way to brittels on the other side, shaped like flat plates for protection, but with planty stems that crept out and around the sides and up toward the sunlight.

Wyndle sniffed, crossing to the ground beside her. "Barely any cultivation. Why, this is no garden. Whoever maintains this should be reprimanded."

"I like it," Lift said, lifting her hand toward some lifespren, which bobbed over her fingertips. The garden was crowded with people. Some were coming and going, while others lounged about, and still others begged for chips. She hadn't seen many beggars in the city; likely there were all *kinds* of rules and regulations about when you could do it and how.

She stopped, hands on hips. "People here, in Azir and Tashikk, they *love* to write stuff down."

"Oh, most certainly," Wyndle said, curling around some vines. "Mmm. Yes, mistress, these at least are fruit vines. I suppose that is better; it's not *completely* haphazard."

"And they love information," Lift said. "They love tradin' it with one another, right?"

"Most certainly. That is a distinguishing factor of their cultural identity, as your tutors said in the palace. You weren't there. I went to listen in your place."

"What people write can be important, at least to them," Lift said. "But what would they do with it all when they're done with it? Throw it out? Burn it?"

"Throw it out? Mother's vines! No, no, no. You can't just go throwing things out! They might be useful later on. If it were me, I'd find someplace safe for them, and keep them pristine in case I needed them!"

Lift nodded, folding her arms. They'd have his same attitude. This city, with everyone writing notes and rules, then offering to sell everyone else ideas all the time . . . Well, in some ways this place was like a *whole city* of Wyndles.

Darkness had told his hunters to find someone who was doing strange stuff. Awesome stuff. And in this city they wrote down what kids had for *breakfast*.

If somebody had seen something strange, they'd have written it down.

Lift scampered through the garden, brushing vines with her toes and causing them to writhe away. She hopped up onto a bench beside a likely target, an older woman in a brown shiqua, with the head portions pulled up and down to show a middle-aged face wearing makeup and displaying hints of styled hair.

The woman wrinkled her nose immediately, which was unfair. Lift had taken a bath back a week or so in Azir, and it had had soap and everything.

"Shoo," the woman said, waving fingers at her. "I've no money for you. Shoo. Go away."

"Don't want money," Lift said. "I've got a *deal* to make. For information."

"I want nothing from you."

"I can give you nothing," Lift said, relaxing. "I'm good at that. I'll go away, and give you nothing. You just gotta answer a question for me."

Lift hunched there on the bench, not moving. Then she scratched herself on the behind. The woman fussed, looking like she was going to leave, and Lift leaned in.

"You are disobeying beggar regulations," the woman snapped.

"Ain't beggin'. I'm tradin'."

"Fine. What do you want to know?"

"Is there a place," Lift said, "in this city where people stuff all the things they wrote down, to keep them safe?"

The woman frowned, then raised her hand and pointed along a street, which led straight for a distance, toward a moundlike bunker that rose from the center of the city. It was big enough to tower over the rest of the stuff around it, peeking up above the tops of the trenches.

"You mean like the Grand Indicium?" the woman asked.

Lift blinked, then cocked her head.

The woman took the opportunity to flee to a different part of the garden.

"Has that always been there?" Lift asked.

"Um, yes," Wyndle said. "Of course it has."

"Really?" Lift scratched her head. "Huh."

12

Wyndle's vines wove up the side of an alleyway, and Lift climbed, not caring if she drew attention. She hauled herself over the top edge into a field where farmers watched the sky and grumbled. The seasons had gone insane. It was supposed to be raining constantly—a bad time to plant, as the water would wash away the seed paste.

Yet it hadn't rained for days. No storms, no water. Lift walked along, passing farmers who spread paste that would grow to tiny polyps, which would eventually grow to the size of large rocks and fill to bursting with grain. Mash that grain—either by hand or by storm—and it made new paste. Lift had always wondered why she didn't grow polyps inside her stomach after eating, and nobody had ever given her a straight answer.

The confused farmers worked with their shiquas

pulled up to their waists. Lift passed, and she tried to listen. To hear.

This was supposed to be their one time of year where they didn't have to work. Sure, they planted some treb to grow in cracks, as it could survive flooding. But they weren't supposed to have to plant lavis, tallew, or clema: much more labor-intensive—but also more profitable—crops to cultivate.

Yet here they were. What if it rained tomorrow, and washed away all this effort? What if it never rained again? The city cisterns, which were glutted with water from the weeks of Weeping, would not last forever. They were so worried, she caught sight of some fearspren—shaped like globs of purple goo—gathering around the mounds upon which the men planted.

As a counterpoint, lifespren broke off from the growing polyps and bobbed over to Lift, trailing in her wake. A swirling, green-glowing dust. Ahead of her, the Grand Indicium rose like the head of a bald man seen peeking above the back of the chair he was sitting in. It was a huge rounded mass of stone.

Everything in the city revolved around this central point. Streets turned in this direction, curling up to it, and as Lift drew close, she could see that an enormous swath of stone had been cut away around the Indicium. The round bunker wasn't much to look at, but it sure did seem secure from the storms.

"Yes, the land *does* slope away from this central point," Wyndle noted. "This focus had to be the highest point of the city anyway—and I guess they figured they'd just accept that, and make the central knob into a fortress."

A fortress for books. People could be so strange. Below, crowds of people—most of them Tashikki—flowed in and out of the building, which had numerous screwlike sloped walkways leading up to it.

Lift settled down on the edge of the wall, feet hanging over. "Kinda looks like the tip of some guy's dangly bits. Like some fellow had such a short sword, everyone felt so sorry for him they said, 'Hey, we'll make a *huge* statue to it, and even though it's tiny, it'll look real big!'"

Wyndle sighed.

"That wasn't crude," Lift noted. "That was being poetic. Ol' Whitehair said you can't be crass, so long as you're talkin' 'bout art. Then you're being elegant. That's why it's okay to hang pictures of naked ladies in a palace."

"Mistress, wasn't this the man who got himself *intentionally* swallowed by a Marabethian greatshell?"

"Yup. Crazy as a box full of drunk minks, that one. I miss him." She liked to pretend he hadn't actually gotten eaten. He'd winked at her as he'd jumped into the greatshell's gaping maw, shocking the crowd.

Wyndle piled around on himself, forming a face—eyes made of crystals, lips formed of a tiny network of vines. "Mistress, what is our plan?"

"Plan?"

He sighed. "We need to get into that building. Are you just going to do whatever strikes you?"

"Obviously."

"Might I offer some suggestions?"

"Long as it doesn't involve sucking someone's soul, Voidbringer."

"I'm not— Look, mistress, that building is an archive. Knowing what I do of this region, the rooms in there will be filled with laws, records, and reports. Thousands upon thousands upon thousands of them."

"Yeah," she said, making a fist. "Among all that, they'll have written down strange stuff for sure!"

"And how, precisely, are we going to find the specific information we want?"

"Easy. You're gonna read it."

". . . Read it."

"Yup. We'll get in there, you'll read their books and stuff, and then we'll decide where strange events were. That will lead us to Darkness's lunch."

". . . Read it *all*."

"Yup."

"Do you have any idea how much information is likely held in that place?" Wyndle said. "There will be hundreds of thousands of reports and ledgers. And to state it explicitly, yes, that's a number more than ten, so you can't count to it."

"I'm not an idiot," she snapped. "I got toes too."

"It's still far more than I can read. I can't sift through all of that information for you. It's impossible. Not going to happen."

She eyed him. "All right. Maybe I can get you *one* soul. Perhaps a tax collector . . . 'cept they ain't human. Would they work? Or would you need, like, three of them to make up one normal person's soul?"

"Mistress! I'm not *bargaining*!"

"Come on. Everyone knows Voidbringers like a good deal. Does it have to be someone important? Or can it be some dumb guy nobody likes?"

"I don't *eat souls*," Wyndle exclaimed. "I'm not trying to haggle with you! I'm stating facts. I *can't read* all the information in that archive! Why can't you just see that—"

"Oh, calm your tentacles," Lift said, swinging her feet, bouncing her heels against the rock cliff. "I hear you. Can't help but hear you, considering how much you whine."

Behind, the farmers were asking whose daughter she was, and why she wasn't running them water like kids were supposed to. Lift scrunched up her face, thinking. "Can't wait until night and sneak in," she muttered.

"Darkness wants the poor person killed by then. 'Sides, I bet those scribes work nights. They feed off ink. Why sleep when you could be writin' up some new law about how many fingers people can use to hold a spoon?

"They know their stuff though. They sell it all over the place. The viziers were always writing to them to get some answer to something. Mostly news around the world." She grinned, then stood up. "You're right. We gotta do this differently."

"Yes indeed."

"We gotta be *smart* about it. *Devious.* Think like a Voidbringer."

"I didn't say—"

"Stop complaining," Lift said. "I'm gonna go steal some important-looking clothes."

13

Lift liked soft clothing. These supple Azish coat and robes were the wardrobe equivalent of silky pudding. It was good to remember that life wasn't only about scratchy things. Sometimes it was about soft pillows, fluffy cake. Nice words. Mothers.

The world couldn't be completely bad when it had soft clothes. This outfit was big for her, but that was okay. She liked it loose. She snuggled into the robes, sitting in the chair, crossing her hands in her lap, wearing a cap on her head. The entire costume was marked by bright colors woven in patterns that meant very important things. She was pretty sure of that, because everyone in Azir wouldn't shut up about their patterns.

The scribe was fat. She needed, like, three shiquas to cover her. Either that or a shiqua made for a horse. Lift wouldn't have thought that they'd give scribes so much food. What did they need so much energy for? Pens were really light.

The woman wore spectacles and kept her face covered, despite being in lands that knew Tashi. She tapped her pen against the table. "*You're* from the palace in Azir."

"Yup," Lift said. "Friend of the emperor. I call him Gawx, but they changed his name to something else. Which is okay, because Gawx is kind of a dumb name, and you don't want your emperor to sound dumb." She cocked her head. "Can't stop that if he starts talking though."

On the ground beside her, Wyndle groaned softly.

"Did you know," Lift said, leaning in to the scribe, "that they've got someone who *picks his nose* for him?"

"Young lady, I believe you are wasting my time."

"That's pretty insulting," Lift said, sitting up straight in her seat, "considering how little you people seem to do around here."

It was true. This whole building was full of scribes rushing this way and that, carrying piles of paper to one windowless alcove or another. They even had this spren that hung out here, one Lift had only seen a couple of times. It looked like little ripples in the air, like a raindrop in a pond—only without the rain, and without the pond. Wyndle called them concentrationspren.

Anyway, they had so much starvin' paper in the place that they needed parshmen to cart it about for them! One passed in the hallway outside, a woman carrying a large box of papers. Those would be hauled to one of a billion scribes who sat at tables, surrounded by blinking spanreeds. Wyndle said they were answering inquiries from around the world, passing information.

The scribe with Lift was a slightly more important one. Lift had gotten into the room by doing as Wyndle suggested: not talking. The viziers did that kind of thing too. Nodding, not saying anything. She'd presented the card, where she'd sketched the words that Wyndle had formed for her with vines.

The people at the front had been intimidated enough to lead her through the hallways to this room, which was larger than others—but it still didn't have any windows. The wall had a brownish yellow stain on the white paint though, and you could pretend it was sunlight.

On the other wall was a shelf that held a really long rack of spanreeds. A few Azish tapestries hung at the back. This scribe was some kind of liaison with the government over in Azir.

Once in the room though, Lift had been forced to talk. She couldn't avoid that anymore. She just needed to be persuasive.

"What unfortunate person," the large scribe asked, "did you mug to get that clothing?"

"Like I'd take it off someone while they were *wearing* it," Lift said, rolling her eyes. "Look. Just pull out one of those glowing pens and write to the palace. Then we can get on to the important stuff. My Voidbringer says you got *tons* of papers in here we're gonna have to look through."

The woman stood up. Lift could practically hear her chair breathe a sigh of relief. The woman pointed toward the door dismissively, but at that moment a lesser scribe—spindly, and wearing a yellow shiqua and a strange brown and yellow cap—entered and whispered in the woman's ear.

She looked displeased. The newcomer shrugged awkwardly, then hurried back out. The fat woman turned to eye Lift. "Give me the names of the viziers you know in the palace."

"Well, there's Dalky—she's got a funny nose, like a spigot. And Big A, I can't say his real name. It's got those choking sounds in it. And Daddy Sag-butt, he's not really a vizier. They call him a scion, which is a different kind of important. Oh! And Fat Lips! She's in charge of them. She doesn't really have fat lips, but she hates it when I call her that."

The woman stared at Lift. Then she turned and walked to the door. "Wait here." She stepped outside.

Lift leaned over toward the ground. "How'm I doin'?"

"Terribly," Wyndle said.

"Yeah. I noticed."

"It's almost as if," Wyndle said, "it would have been *useful* to learn how to talk politely, like the viziers kept telling you."

"Blah blah," Lift said, going to the door and listening. Outside, she could faintly hear the scribes talking.

"... matches the description given by the captain of the immigration watch to search for in the city..." one of them said. "She showed up right here! We've sent to the captain, who luckily is here for her debriefing..."

"Damnation," Lift whispered, pulling back. "They're on to us, Voidbringer."

"I should never have helped you with this insane idea!"

Lift crossed the room to the racks of spanreeds. They were all labeled. "Get over here and tell me which one we need."

Wyndle grew up the wall and sent vines across the nameplates. "My, my. These are important reeds. Let's see ... third one over, it will go to the royal palace scribes."

"Great," Lift said, grabbing it and scrambling onto

the table. She set it into the right spot on the board—she'd seen this done tons of times—and twisted the ruby on the top of the reed. It was answered immediately; palace scribes weren't often away from their reeds. They'd sooner give up their fingers.

Lift grabbed the spanreed and placed it against the paper. "Uh . . ."

"Oh, for Cultivation's sake," Wyndle said. "You didn't pay attention at all, did you?"

"Nope."

"Tell me what you want to say."

She said it out, and he again made vines grow across the table in the right shapes. Pen gripped in her fist, she copied the words, one stupid letter at a time. It took *forever*. Writing was ridiculous. Couldn't people just talk? Why invent a way where you didn't have to actually see people to tell them what to do?

This is Lift, she wrote. *Tell Fat Lips I need her. I'm in trouble. And somebody get Gawx. If he's not having his nose picked right—*

The door opened and Lift yelped, twisting the ruby and scrambling off the table.

Beyond the door was a large gathering of people. Five scribes, including the fat one, and three guards. One was the woman who ran the guard post into the city.

Storms, Lift thought. *That was fast.*

She ducked toward them.

"Careful!" the guard shouted. "She's slippery!"

Lift made herself awesome, but the guard shoved the scribes into the room and started pushing the door shut behind her. Lift got between their legs, Slick and sliding easily, but slammed right into the door as it closed.

The guard lunged for her. Lift yelped, coating herself with awesomeness so that when she got grabbed, her wide-sleeved Azish coat came off, leaving her in a robelike skirt with trousers underneath, and then her normal shirts.

She scuttled across the ground, but the room wasn't large. She tried to scramble around the perimeter, but the guard captain was right on her.

"Mistress!" Wyndle cried. "Oh, mistress. Don't get stabbed! Are you listening? Avoid getting hit by anything sharp! Or blunt, actually!"

Lift growled as the other guards slipped in, then quickly shut the door. One prowled around on either side of the room.

She dodged one way, then the other, then punched at the shelf with the spanreeds, causing the scribe to scream as several toppled over.

Lift bolted for the door. The guard captain tackled her, and another piled on top of *her*.

Lift squirmed, making herself awesome, squeezing through their fingers. She just had to—

"Tashi," a scribe whispered. "God of Gods and Binder of the World!" Awespren, like a ring of blue smoke, burst out around her head.

Lift popped out of the grips of the guards, stepping up to stand on one of their backs, which gave her a good view of the desk. The spanreed was writing.

"Took them long enough," she said, then hopped off the guards and sat in the chair.

The guard stood up behind her, cursing.

"Stop, Captain!" the fat scribe said. She looked at the spindly scribe in yellow. "Go get another spanreed to the Azish palace. Get two! We need confirmation."

"For what?" the scribe said, walking to the desk. The guard captain joined them, reading what the pen wrote.

Then, slowly, all three looked up at Lift with wide eyes.

" 'To whom it may concern,' " Wyndle read, spreading his vines up onto the table over the paper. " 'It is decreed that I—Prime Aqasix Yanagawn the First, emperor of all Makabak—proclaim that the young woman known as Lift is to be shown every courtesy and measure of respect.

" 'You will obey her as you would myself, and bill to the imperial account any charges that might be incurred by her . . . foray in your city. What follows is a description of the woman, and two questions only she can answer, as proof of authentication. But know this—if she is harmed or impeded in any way, you will know imperial wrath.'"

"Thanks, Gawx," Lift said, then looked up at the scribes and guards. "That means you gotta do what I say!"

"And . . . what is it you want?" the fat scribe asked.

"Depends," Lift said. "What were you going to have for lunch today?"

14

Three hours later, Lift sat in the center of the fat scribe's desk, eating pancakes with her hands and wearing the spindly scribe's hat.

A swarm of lesser scribes searched through reports on the ground in front of her, piles of books scattered about like broken crab shells after a fine feast. The fat scribe stood beside the desk, reading to Lift from the spanreed that wrote Gawx's end of their conversation. The woman had finally pulled down her face wrap, and it turned out she was pretty and a lot younger than Lift had assumed.

"'I'm worried, Lift,'" the fat scribe read to her. "'*Every-one* here is worried. There are reports coming in from the west now. Steen and Alm have seen the new storm. It's happening like the Alethi warlord said it would. A storm of red lightning, blowing the wrong direction.'"

The woman looked up at Lift. "He's right about that, um . . ."

"Say it," Lift said.

"Your Pancakefulness."

"Rolls right off the tongue, doesn't it?"

"His Imperial Excellency is correct about the arrival of a strange new storm. We have independent confirmation of that from contacts in Shinovar and Iri. An enormous storm with red lightning, blowing in from the west."

"And the monsters?" Lift said. "Things with red eyes in the darkness?"

"Everything is in chaos," the scribe said—her name was Ghenna. "We've had trouble getting straight answers. We had some inkling of this, from reports on the east coast when the storm struck there, before blowing into the ocean. Most people thought those reports exaggerated, and that the storm would blow itself out. Now that it has rounded the planet and struck in the west . . . Well, the prince is reportedly preparing a diktat of emergency for the entire country."

Lift looked at Wyndle, who was coiled on the desk beside her. "Voidbringers," he said, voice small. "It's happening. Sweet virtue . . . the Desolations *have* returned. . . ."

Ghenna went back to reading the spanreed from Gawx. "'This is going to be a disaster, Lift. Nobody is ready for a storm that blows the wrong direction. Almost as bad, though, are the Alethi. How do the Alethi know so much about it? Did that warlord of theirs summon it somehow?'" Ghenna lowered the paper.

Lift chewed on her pancake. It was a dense variety, with mashed-up paste in the center that was too sticky and salty. The one beside it was covered in little crunchy seeds. Neither were as good as the other two varieties she'd tried over the last few hours.

"When's it going to hit?" Lift asked.

"The storm? It's hard to judge, but it's slower than a highstorm, by most reports. It might arrive in Azir and Tashikk in three or four hours."

"Write this to Gawx," Lift said around bites of pancake. "'They got good food here. These pancakes, with lots of variety. One has sugar in the center.'"

The scribe hesitated.

"Write it," Lift said. "Or I'll make you call me more silly names."

Ghenna sighed, but complied.

"'Lift,'" she read as the spanreed wrote the next line from Gawx, who undoubtedly had about fifteen viziers and scions standing around telling him what to say, then writing it when he agreed. "'This isn't the time for idle conversation about food.'"

"Sure it is," Lift replied. "We gotta remember. Storm

might be coming, but people will still need to eat. The world ends tomorrow, but the day after that, people are going to ask what's for breakfast. That's your job."

" 'And what about the stories of something worse?' " he wrote back. " 'The Alethi are warning about parshmen, and I'm doing what I can on such short notice. But what of the Voidbringers they say are in the storms?' "

Lift looked at the room packed with scribes. "I'm workin' on that part," she said. As Ghenna wrote it, Lift stood up, wiping her hands on her fancy robes. "Hey, all you smart people. Whatcha found?"

The scribes looked up at her. "Mistress," one said, "we don't have *any* idea what we're even looking for."

"Strange stuff!"

"What kind of 'strange stuff'?" asked the scribe in yellow, the spindly fellow who looked silly and balding without a hat. "Unusual things happen every day in the city! Do you want the report of the man who claims his pig was born with two heads? What about the man who says he saw the shape of Yaezir in the lichen on his wall? The woman who had a premonition her sister would fall, and then she fell?"

"Nah," Lift said. "That's *normal* strange."

"What's abnormal strange, then?" he asked, exasperated.

Lift started glowing. She called upon her awesomeness, so much that it started radiating out of her skin, like she was a starvin' sphere.

Beside her, the seeds on top of her uneaten pancake sprouted, growing long, twisting vines that curled around one another and spat out leaves.

"Somethin' like this," Lift said, then glanced to the side. Great. She'd ruined the pancake.

The scribes stared at her in awe, so she clapped loudly, sending them back to their work. Wyndle sighed, and she knew what he must be thinking. Three hours, and nothing relevant so far. He'd been right—yeah, they wrote stuff down in this city. That was the problem. They wrote it *all* down.

"There's another message from the emperor for you," Ghenna said. "Um, Your Pancake . . . Storms that sounds stupid."

Lift grinned, then looked over at the paper. The words were written in a flowing, elegant hand. Probably Fat Lips.

" 'Lift,' " Ghenna read. " 'Are you going to come back? We miss you here.' "

"Even Fat Lips?" Lift asked.

" 'Vizier Noura misses you too. Lift, this is your home now. You don't need to live on the streets anymore.' "

"What am I supposed to do there, if I do come back?"

" 'Anything you want,' " Gawx wrote. " 'I promise.' "

That was the problem.

"I don't know what I'm gonna do yet," she said, feeling strangely . . . isolated, despite the roomful of people. "We'll see."

Ghenna eyed her at that. She apparently thought that what the emperor of Azir wanted, he should get—and little Reshi girls shouldn't make a habit of denying him.

The door cracked open, and the guard captain from the city watch peeked in. Lift leaped off the desk, running over to her, then hopping up to see what she was holding. A report. Great. More words.

"What did you find?" Lift said eagerly.

"You are right," the captain said. "One of my colleagues in the quarter's watch has been watching the Tashi's Light Orphanage. The woman who runs it—"

"The Stump," Lift said. "Meanest thing. Eats the bones of children for afternoon snack. Once had a staring contest with a painting and won."

"—is being investigated. She's running some kind of money-laundering scheme, though the details are confusing. She's been seen trading spheres for ones of lesser value, a practice that would end with her bankrupt, if she didn't have another income scheme. The report says she takes money from criminal enterprises as donations, then secretly transfers them to other groups, after taking a cut, to help confuse the trail of spheres. There's more too. In any case, the children are a front to keep attention away from her practices."

"I told you," Lift said, snatching the paper. "You should arrest her and spend all her money on soup. Give me half, for tellin' you where to look, and I won't tell nobody."

The guard raised her eyebrows.

"We can write down that we did it, if you want," Lift said. "That'll make it *official.*"

"I'll ignore the suggestions of bribery, coercion, extortion, and state embezzlement," the captain said. "As for the orphanage, I don't have jurisdiction over it, but I assure you my colleagues will be moving against this . . . Stump soon."

"Good enough," Lift said, climbing back up on the desk before her legion of scribes. "So what have you found? Anybody glowing, like they're some stormin' benevolent force for good or some such crem?"

"This is too large a project to spring on us without warning!" the fat scribe complained. "Mistress, this is the sort of research we normally have *months* to work on. Give us three weeks, and we can prepare a detailed report!"

"We ain't got three weeks. We barely got three hours."

It didn't matter. Over the next few hours, she tried cajoling, threatening, dancing, bribing, and—as a last-ditch, crazy option—remaining perfectly quiet and letting them read. As the time slipped away, they found nothing and everything at the same time. There were *tons* of vague oddities in the guard reports: stories of a man surviving a fall from too high, a complaint of strange noises outside a woman's window, spren acting odd every morning outside a woman's house unless she left out a bowl of sugar water. Yet none of them had more than one witness, and in each case the guard had found nothing specifically strange other than hearsay.

Each time a weirdness came up, Lift itched to scramble out the door, squeeze through a window, and go running to find the person involved. Each time, Wyndle cautioned patience. If all these reports were true, then basically every person in the city would have been a Surgebinder. What if she ran off chasing one of the hundred reports that were due to ordinary superstition? She'd spend hours and find nothing.

Which was exactly what she felt like she was doing. She was annoyed, impatient, *and* out of pancakes.

"I'm sorry, mistress," Wyndle said as they rejected a report about a Veden woman who claimed her baby had been "blessed by Tashi Himself to have lighter skin than his father, to make him more comfortable interacting with foreigners."

"I don't think any of these is more likely a sign than the one before. I'm beginning to feel we just need to pick one and hope we get lucky."

Lift hated luck, these days. She was having trouble convincing herself that she hadn't hit an unlucky age of her life, so she'd given up on luck. She'd even traded her lucky sphere for a piece of hog's cheese.

The more she thought of it, the more that *luck* seemed the opposite of being *awesome*. One was something you did; the other was something that happened to you no matter what you did.

Course, that didn't mean luck didn't exist. You either believed in that, or you believed in what those Vorin priests were always saying—that poor people was *chosen* to be poor, on account of them being too dumb to ask the Almighty to make them born with heaps of spheres.

"So what do we do?" Lift said.

"Pick one of these accounts, I guess," Wyndle said. "Any of them. Except maybe that one about the baby. I suspect that the mother might not be honest."

"Ya think?"

Lift looked over the papers spread before her— papers she couldn't read, each detailing a report of some vague curiosity. Storms. Pick the right one and she could save a life, maybe find someone else who could do what she did.

Pick the wrong one, and Darkness or his servants would execute an innocent. Quietly, with nobody to witness their passing or to remember them.

Darkness. She hated him, suddenly. With a seething ferocity that startled even her with its intensity. She didn't think she'd ever actually *hated* anyone before. Him though . . . those cold eyes that seemed to refuse all emotion. She hated him more for the fact that it seemed like he did what he did without a shred of guilt.

"Mistress?" Wyndle asked. "What do you choose?"

"I can't choose," she whispered. "I don't know how."

"Just pick one."

"I can't. I don't make choices, Wyndle."

"Nonsense! You do it every day."

"No. I just . . ." She went where the winds blew. Once you made a decision, you were committed. You were saying you thought this was *right*.

The door to their chamber was flung open. A guard there, one Lift didn't recognize, was sweating and puffing. "Status Five emergency diktat from the prince, to be disseminated through the nation immediately. State of emergency in the city. Storm blowing from the wrong direction, projected to hit within two hours.

"All people are to get off the streets and go to storm bunkers, and parshmen are to be imprisoned or exiled into the storm. He wants the alleys of Yeddaw and slot cities evacuated, and orders government officials to report to their assigned bunkers to do head counts, draft reports, and mediate confusion or evacuation disputes. Find a draft of these orders posted at each muster station, with copies being distributed now."

The scribes in the room looked up from their work, then immediately began packing away books and ledgers.

"Wait!" Lift said as the runner moved on. "What are you doing?"

"You've just gotten overruled, little one," Ghenna said. "Your research will have to be put on hold."

"How long!"

"Until the prince decides to step down our state of emergency," she said, quickly gathering the spanreeds from her shelf and packing them in a padded case.

"But, the emperor!" Lift said, grabbing a note from Gawx and wagging it. "He said to help me!"

"We'll gladly help you to a storm bunker," the guard captain said.

"I need help with this problem! He *ordered* you to obey!"

"We, of course, listen to the emperor," Ghenna said. "We will listen very well."

But not necessarily obey. The viziers had explained this. Azir might *claim* to be an empire, and most of the other countries in the region played along. Just like you might play along with the kid who says he's team captain during a game of rings. As soon as his demands grew too extravagant though, he might find himself talking to an empty alleyway.

The scribes were remarkably efficient. It wasn't too long before they'd ushered Lift into the hallway, burdened her with a handful of reports she couldn't read, then split to run to their various duties. They left her with one junior sub-scribe who couldn't be much older than Lift; her job was to show Lift to a storm bunker.

Lift ditched the girl at the first junction she could, scuttling down a side path as the girl explained the emergency to a bleary-eyed old scholar in a brown shiqua. Lift stripped off her nice Azish clothing and dumped it in a corner, leaving her in trousers, shirt, and unbuttoned overshirt. From there she set off into a less-populated section of the building. In the large corridors, scribes gathered and shouted at one another. She wouldn't have expected such a ruckus from a bunch of dried-up old men and women with ink for blood.

It was dark in here, and Lift found reason to wish she hadn't traded away her lucky sphere. The hallways were marked by rugs with Azish patterns to differentiate them, but that was about it. Periodic sphere lanterns lined the walls, but only every fifth one had an infused sphere in it. Everyone was still starvin' for Stormlight. She spent a good minute holding to one, chewing on its latch and trying to get it undone, but they were locked up tight.

She continued down the hallway, passing room after room, each stuffed with paper—though there weren't as many bookshelves as Lift had expected to find. It wasn't like a library. Instead there were walls full of drawers that you could pull open to find stacks of pages.

The longer she walked the quieter it became, until it was like she was walking through a mausoleum—for trees. She crinkled up the papers in her hand and shoved them in her pocket. There were so many, she couldn't properly get her hand in as well.

"Mistress?" Wyndle said from the floor beside her. "We don't have much time."

"I'm thinkin'," Lift said. Which was a lie. She was trying to *avoid* thinkin'.

"I'm sorry the plan didn't work," Wyndle said.

Lift shrugged. "You don't want to be here anyway. You want to be off gardening."

"Yes, I had the most lovely gallery of boots planned," Wyndle said. "But I suppose . . . I suppose we can't sit around preparing gardens while the world ends, can we? And if I'd been placed with that nice Iriali, I wouldn't be here, would I? And that Radiant you're trying to save, they'd be as good as dead."

"Probably as good as dead anyway."

"But still . . . still worth trying, right?"

Stupid cheerful Voidbringer. She glanced at him, then pulled out the wads of paper. "These are useless. We gotta start over with a new plan."

"And with much less time. Sunset is coming, along with that storm. What do we do?"

Lift dropped the papers. "Somebody knows where to go. That woman who was talkin' to Darkness, his apprentice, she said she had an investigation going. Sounded confident."

"Huh," Wyndle said. "You don't suppose her investigation involved . . . a bunch of scribes searching records, do you?"

Lift cocked her head.

"That would be the smart thing to do," Wyndle said. "I mean, even *we* came up with it."

Lift grinned, then ran back in the direction she'd come from.

15

Yes," the fat scribe said, flustered after looking through a book. "It was Bidlel's team, room two-three-two. The woman you describe hired them two weeks ago for an undisclosed project. We take the secrecy of our clients *very* seriously." She sighed, closing the book. "Barring imperial mandate."

"Thanks," Lift said, giving the woman a hug. "Thanksthanksthanksthanks."

"I wish I knew what all this meant. Storms . . . you'd think I would be the one who got told everything, but half the time I get the sense that even kings are confused by what the world throws at them." She shook her head and looked to Lift, who was still hugging her. "I *am* going to my assigned station now. You'd be wise to seek shelter."

"Surewillgreatbye," Lift said, letting go and dashing out of the room full of ledgers. She scurried through the hallway, directly *away* from the steps down to the Indicium's storm shelter.

Ghenna poked her head out into the hallway. "Bidlel will have already evacuated! The door will be locked." She paused. "Don't break anything!"

"Voidbringer," Lift said, "can you find whatever number she just said?"

"Yes."

"Good. 'Cuz I don't got that many toes."

They hurried through the cavernous Indicium, which was already feeling empty. Only a half hour or so since the diktat—Wyndle was keeping track—and everyone was on their way out. People locked the doors in the advent of a storm, and moved on to safe places. For those with regular homes, those homes would do, but for the poor that meant storm bunkers.

Poor parshmen. There weren't many in the city, not as many as in Azimir, but by the prince's orders they were being gathered and turned out. Left for the storm, which Lift considered hugely unfair.

Nobody listened to her complaints about that though. And Wyndle implied . . . well, they might be turning into Voidbringers. And he would know.

Still didn't seem fair. She wouldn't leave *him* out in a storm. Even if he claimed it probably wouldn't hurt them.

She followed Wyndle's vines as he led her up two floors, then started counting off rows. The floor on this level was of painted wood, and it felt weird to walk on it. Wooden floors. Wouldn't they break and fall through? Wooden buildings always felt so flimsy to her, and she stepped lightly just in case. It—

Lift frowned, then crouched down, looking one way, then the other. What was that?

"Two-Two-One . . ." Wyndle said. "Two-Two-Two . . ."

"Voidbringer!" Lift hissed. "Shut up."

He twisted about, creeping up the wall near her. Lift pressed her back against the wall, then ducked around a corner into a side corridor and pressed her back against that wall instead.

Booted feet thumped on the carpet. "I can't believe you call *that* a lead," a woman's voice said. Lift recognized it as Darkness's trainee. "Weren't you in the guard?"

"Things work differently in Yezier," a man snapped. The other trainee. "Here, everyone is too coy. They should just say what they mean."

"You expect a Tashikki street informant to be *perfectly clear*?"

"Sure. Isn't that his job?"

The two strode past, and thankfully didn't glance down the side hall toward Lift. Storms, those uniforms—with the high boots, stiff Eastern jackets, and large-cuffed gloves—were imposing. They looked like generals on the field.

Lift itched to follow and see where they went. She forced herself to wait.

Sure enough, a few seconds later a quieter figure passed in the hallway. The assassin, clothing tattered, head bowed, with that large sword—it *had* to be some kind of Shardblade—resting on his shoulder.

"I do not know, sword-nimi," he said softly, "I don't trust my own mind any longer." He paused, stopping as if listening to something. "That is not comforting, sword-nimi. No, it is not. . . ."

He trailed after the other two, leaving a faint afterimage glowing in the air. It was almost imperceptible, less pronounced now that he was moving than it had been in Darkness's headquarters.

"Oh, mistress," Wyndle said, curling up to her. "I nearly expired of fright! The way he stopped there in the hallway, I was *sure* he'd seen me somehow!"

At least the hallways were dark, with those sphere lanterns mostly out. Lift nervously slipped into the hallway and followed the group. They stopped at the right door, and one produced a key. Lift had expected them to ransack the place, but of course they wouldn't need to do that—they had legal authority.

Actually, so did she. How bizarre.

Darkness's two apprentices stepped into the room.

The Assassin in White remained outside in the hall-way. He settled down on the floor across from the doorway, his strange Shardblade across his lap. He sat mostly still, but when he did move, he left that fading afterimage behind.

Lift pulled into the side corridor again, back pressed to the wall. People shouted somewhere distant in the Grand Indecision, calls for people to be orderly.

"I have to get into that room," Lift said. "Somehow."

Wyndle huddled down on the ground, vines tight-ening around him.

Lift shook her head. "That means getting past the starvin' *assassin* himself. Storms."

"I'll do it," Wyndle whispered.

"Maybe," Lift said, barely paying attention, "I can make some sorta distraction. Send him off chasin' it? But then that would alert the two in the room."

"I'll do it," Wyndle repeated.

Lift cocked her head, registering what he'd said. She glanced down at him. "The distraction?"

"No." Wyndle's vines twisted about one another, tightening into knots. "I'll do it, mistress. I can sneak into the room. I . . . I don't believe their spren will be able to see me."

"You don't know?"

"No."

"Sounds dangerous."

His vines scrunched as they tightened against one another. "You think?"

"Yeah, totally," Lift said, then peeked around the corner. "Something's wrong about that guy in white. Can you get killed, Voidbringer?"

"Destroyed," Wyndle said. "Yes. It's not the same as for a human, but I have . . . seen spren who . . ." He whimpered softly. "Maybe it *is* too dangerous for me."

"Maybe."

Wyndle settled down, coiled about himself.

"I'm going anyway," he whispered.

She nodded. "Just listen, memorize what those two in there say, and get back here quick. If something happens, scream loud as you can."

"Right. Listen and scream. I can listen and scream. I'm good at these things." He made a sound like taking a deep breath, though so far as she knew he didn't need to breathe. Then he shot out into the corridor, a vine laced with crystal that grew along the corner where wall met floor. Little offshoots of green crept off his sides, covering the carpeting.

The assassin didn't look up. Wyndle reached the doorway into the room with the two Skybreaker apprentices. Lift couldn't hear a word of what was being said inside.

Storms, she hated waiting. She'd built her life around not having to wait for anyone or anything. She did what she wanted, when she wanted. That was the best, right? Everyone should be able to do what they wanted.

Of course if they did that, who would grow food? If the world was full of people like Lift, wouldn't they just leave halfway through planting to go catch lurgs? Nobody would protect the streets, or sit around in meetings. Nobody would learn to write things down, or make kingdoms run. Everyone would scurry about eating each other's food, until it was all gone and the whole heap of them fell over and *died.*

You knew that, a part of her said, standing up inside, hands on hips with a defiant attitude. *You knew the truth of the world even when you went and asked not to get older.*

Being young was an excuse. A plausible justification.

She waited, feeling itchy because she couldn't do anything. What were they saying in there? Had they spotted Wyndle? Were they torturing him? Threatening to . . . cut down his gardens or something?

Listen, a part of her whispered.

But of course she couldn't hear anything.

She wanted to just rush in there, make faces at them all, then drag them on a chase through the starvin' building. That would be better than sitting here with her thoughts, worrying and condemning herself at the same time.

When you were always busy, you didn't have to think about stuff. Like how most people didn't run off and leave when the whim struck them. Like how your mother had been so warm, and kindly, so ready to take care of everyone. It was incredible that anyone on Roshar should be as good to people as she'd been.

She shouldn't have had to die. Least, she should have had someone half as wonderful as she was to take care of her as she wasted away.

Someone other than Lift, who was selfish, stupid.

And lonely.

She tensed up, then prepared to bolt around the corner. Wyndle, however, finally zipped out into the hallway. He grew along the floor at a frantic pace, then rejoined her—leaving a trail of dust by the wall as his discarded vines crumbled.

Darkness's two apprentices left the room a moment later, and Lift pulled back into the side corridor with Wyndle. In the shadows here, she crouched down against the floor, to avoid standing out against the distant light. The woman and man in uniforms strode past a moment later, and didn't even glance down the hallway. Lift relaxed, fingertips brushing Wyndle's vines.

Then the assassin passed by. He stopped, then looked in her direction, hand resting on his sword hilt.

Lift's breath caught. *Don't become awesome. Don't become awesome!* If she used her powers in these shadows, she'd glow and he'd spot her for sure.

All she could do was crouch there as the assassin narrowed his eyes—strangely shaped, like they were too big or something. He reached to a pouch at his belt, then tossed something small and glowing into the hallway. A sphere.

Lift panicked, uncertain if she should scramble away, grow awesome, or just remain still. Fearspren boiled up around her, lit by the sphere as it rolled near her, and she knew—meeting the assassin's gaze—that he could see her.

He pulled his sword out of the sheath a fraction of an inch. Black smoke poured from the blade, dropping toward the floor and pooling at his feet. Lift felt a sudden, terrible nausea.

The assassin studied her, then snapped the sword into its sheath again. Remarkably, he left, following after the other two, that faint afterimage trailing behind him. He didn't speak a word, and his footfalls on the carpet were almost silent—a faint breeze compared to the clomping of the other two, which Lift could still hear farther down the corridor.

In moments, all three of them had entered the stairwell and were gone.

"Storms!" Lift said, flopping backward on the carpet. "Storming Mother of the World and Father of Storms above! He about made me die of fright."

"I know!" Wyndle said. "Did you hear me not-whimpering?"

"No."

"I was too frightened to even make a sound!"

Lift sat up, then mopped the sweat from her brow. "Wow. Okay, well . . . that was something. What did they talk about?"

"Oh!" Wyndle said, as if he'd forgotten completely about his mission. "Mistress, they had an entire study done! Research for weeks to identify oddities in the city."

"Great! What did they determine?"

"I don't know."

Lift flopped back down.

"They talked over a whole lot of things I didn't understand," Wyndle said. "But mistress, *they* know who the person is! They're heading there right now. To perform an execution." He poked at her with a vine. "So . . . maybe we should follow?"

"Yeah, okay," Lift said. "Guess we can do that. Shouldn't be too hard, right?"

16

Turned out it was *way* hard.

She couldn't get too close, as the hallways had grown eerily empty. And there were tons of branching paths, with little side hallways and rooms everywhere. Mix that with the fact that there weren't many spheres on the walls, and it was a real trick to follow the three.

She did it though. She followed them through the whole starvin' place until they reached some doors out into the city. Lift managed to slip out a window near the doors, falling among some plants beside the stairs outside. She huddled there as the three people she'd been tailing stepped out onto the landing overlooking the city.

Storms, but it felt good to be breathing the open air again, though clouds had moved in front of the setting sun. The whole city felt chilly now. In shadow.

And it was empty.

Before, people had been swarming up and down the steps and ramps into the Grand Indishipium. Now they held only a few last-minute stragglers, and even those were rapidly vanishing as they ducked through doorways, seeking shelter.

The assassin turned eyes toward the west. "The storm is coming," he said.

"All the more reason to be quick," the female apprentice said. She took a sphere from her pocket, then held it up before her and sucked in the light. It streamed into her, and she started to glow with awesomeness.

Then she rose into the air.

She rose into the starvin' air itself!

They can fly? Lift thought. *Why in Damnation can't I fly?*

Her companion rose up beside her.

"Coming, assassin?" The woman looked down toward the landing and the man wearing white.

"I've danced that storm once before," he whispered. "On the day I died. No."

"You're never going to make it into the order at this rate."

He remained silent. The two floating people eyed each other, then the man shrugged. The two of them rose higher, then shot out across the city, avoiding the inconvenience of traveling through the trenches.

They could *storming* fly.

"You're the one he's hunting for, aren't you?" the assassin said softly.

Lift winced. Then she stood up and peeked over the side of the landing where the assassin stood. He turned and looked at her.

"I ain't nobody," Lift said.

"He kills nobodies."

"And you don't?"

"I kill kings."

"Which is *totally* better."

He narrowed his eyes at her, then squatted down, sheathed sword held across his shoulders, with hands draped forward. "No. It is not. I hear their screams, their demands, whenever I see shadow. They haunt me, scramble for my mind, wishing to claim my sanity. I fear they've already won, that the man to whom you speak can no longer distinguish what is the voice of a mad raving and what is not."

"Oooookay," Lift said. "But you didn't attack me."

"No. The sword likes you."

"Great. I like the sword too." She glanced at the sky. "Um . . . do you know where they're going?"

"The report described a man who has been spotted vanishing by several people in the city. He will turn down an alleyway, then it will be empty when someone else follows. People have claimed to see his face twisting to become the face of another. My companions believe he is what is called a Lightweaver, and so must be stopped."

"Is that legal?"

"Nin has procured an injunction from the prince, forbidding any use of Surgebinding in the country, save that specifically authorized." He studied Lift. "I believe the Herald's experiences with you were what taught him to go straight to the top, rather than dancing about with local authorities."

Lift traced the direction the other two had gone. That sky was darkening further, an ominous sign.

"He really is wrong, isn't he?" Lift said. "That one you say is a Herald. He says the Voidbringers aren't back, but they are."

"The new storm reveals it," the assassin said. "But . . . who am I to say? I am mad. Then again, I think that the Herald is too. It makes me agree that the minds of men cannot be trusted. That we need something greater to follow, to guide. But not my stone . . . What good is seeking a greater law, when that law can be the whims of a man either stupid or ruthless?"

"Oooookay," Lift said. "Um, you can be crazy all you want. It's fine. I like crazy people. It's real funny when they lick walls and eat rocks and stuff. But before you start dancing, could you tell me where those other two are going?"

"You won't be able to outrun them."

"So no harm in telling me, right?"

The assassin smiled, though the emotion didn't seem to reach his eyes. "The man who can vanish, this presumed Lightweaver, is an old philosopher well known in the immigrant quarter. He sits in a small amphitheater most days, talking to any who will listen. It is near—"

"—the Tashi's Light Orphanage. Storms. I shoulda guessed. He's almost as weird as you are."

"Will you fight them, little Radiant?" the assassin asked. "You, alone, against two journeyman Skybreakers? A Herald waiting in the wings?"

She glanced at Wyndle. "I don't know. But I have to go anyway, don't I?"

17

Lift engaged her awesomeness. She dug deeply into the power, summoning strength, speed, and Slickness. Darkness's people didn't seem to care if they were witnessed flying about, so Lift decided she didn't care about being seen either.

She leaped away from the assassin, Slicking her feet, then landed on the flat ramp beside the steps that wound up the outside of the building. She intended to shoot down toward the city, sliding along the side of the steps.

Of course, she lasted about a second before her feet shot out in two different directions and she slammed onto the stones crotch-first. She cringed at the flash of pain, but didn't have time for much more, as she fell into a tumble before dropping right off the side of the tall steps.

She crunched down to the bottom a few moments

later, landing in a humiliated heap. Her awesomeness prevented her from getting too hurt, so she ignored Wyndle's cries of worry as he climbed down the wall to her. Instead she twisted about, scrambling up onto her hands and knees. Then she took off running toward the slot that would lead her to the orphanage.

She didn't have time to be bad at this! Normal running wouldn't be fast enough. Her enemies were literally *flying.*

She could see, in her mind's eye, how it should be. The entire city sloped away from this central rise with the Grand Indigestion. She should be able to hit a skid, feet Slick, zipping along the mostly empty street. She should be able to slap her hands against walls she passed, outcroppings, buildings, gaining speed with each push.

She should be like an arrow in flight, pointed, targeted, unchecked.

She could see it. But couldn't *do* it. She threw herself into another skid, but again her feet slipped out from under her. This time they went backward and she fell forward, knocking her face against the stone. She saw a flash of white. When she looked up, the empty street wavered in front of her, but her awesomeness soon healed her.

The shadowed street was a major thoroughfare, but it sat forlorn and empty. People had pulled in awnings and street carts, but had left refuse. Those walls crowded her. Everyone knew to stay out of canyons around a storm, or you'd be swept up in floodwaters. They'd gone and built an entire starvin' city in direct, flagrant violation of that.

Behind her in the distance, the sky rumbled. Before that storm hit, a poor, crazy old man was going to get a visit from two self-righteous assassins. She needed to stop it. She *had* to stop it. She couldn't explain why.

Okay, Lift. Be calm. You can be awesome. You've always been awesome, and now you've got this extra awesomeness. Go. You can do it.

She growled and threw herself into a run, then twisted sideways and slid. She *could* and *would*—

This time, she clipped the corner of a wall at an intersection and ended up sprawled on the ground, with feet toward the sky. She knocked her head back against the ground in frustration.

"Mistress?" Wyndle said, curling up to her. "Oh, I do not like the sound of that storm. . . ."

She got up—feeling ashamed and anything *but* awesome—and decided to just run the rest of the way. Her powers did let her run at speed without getting tired, but she could *feel* that it wasn't going to be enough.

It seemed like ages before she stumbled to a stop outside the orphanage, exhaustionspren swirling around her. She'd run out of awesomeness a short time before arriving, and her stomach growled in protest. The amphitheater was empty, of course. Orphanage to her left, built into the solid stones, seats of the little amphitheater in front of her. And beyond it the dark alleyway, wooden shanties and buildings cluttering the view.

The sky had grown dark, though she didn't know whether it was from the advent of dusk or the coming storm.

Deep within the alleyway, Lift heard a low, raw scream of pain. It sent chills up her spine.

Wyndle had been right. The assassin had been right. What was she doing? She couldn't beat two trained and awesome soldiers. She sank down, worn out, right in the middle of the floor of the amphitheater.

"Do we go in?" Wyndle asked from beside her.

"I don't have any power left," Lift whispered. "I used it up running here."

Had that alleyway always felt so . . . deep? With the shadows of the shanties, the draping cloths and jutting planks of wood, the place looked like an extended barricade—with only the narrowest of pathways through. It seemed like an entirely different world from the rest of the city. It was a dark and hidden realm that could exist only in shadows.

She stood up on unsteady feet, then stepped toward the alleyway.

"What are you doing?" a voice shouted.

Lift spun to find the Stump standing in the doorway of the orphanage.

"You're supposed to go to one of the bunkers!" the woman shouted. "Idiot child." She stalked forward and seized Lift by the arm, towing her into the orphanage. "Don't think that just because you're here, I'll take care of you. There's not room for ones like you, and don't give me any pretense about being sick or tired. Everyone's always pretending in order to get at what we have."

Though she said that, she deposited Lift right inside the orphanage, then slammed the large wooden door and threw the bar down. "Be glad I looked out to see who was screaming." She studied Lift, then sighed loudly. "Suppose you'll want some food."

"I have one meal left," Lift said.

"I've half a mind to give it to the other children," the Stump said. "Honestly, after a prank like that. Standing outside screaming? You should have gone to one of the bunkers. If you think that acting forlorn will earn my pity, you are sadly misguided."

She walked off, muttering. The room here, right inside the doors, was large and open, and children sat on mats all round. A single ruby sphere lit them. The children seemed frightened, several holding to one another. One covered his ears and whimpered as thunder sounded outside.

Lift sank down onto an open mat, feeling surreal, out of place. She'd run all the way here, glowing with power, ready to face monsters that flew in the sky. But here . . . here she was just another orphaned urchin.

She closed her eyes, and listened to them.

"I'm frightened. Is the storm going to be long?"

"Why did everyone have to go inside?"

"I miss my mommy."

"What about the gummers in the alley? Will they be all right?"

Their uncertainty thrummed through Lift. She'd been here. After her mother died, she'd been here. She'd been here dozens of times since, in cities all across the land. Places for forgotten children.

She'd sworn an oath to remember people like them. She hadn't *meant* to. It had just kind of happened. Like everything in her life just kind of happened.

"I want control," she whispered.

"Mistress?" Wyndle said.

"Earlier today," she said. "You told me you didn't believe I'd come here for any of the reasons I'd said. You asked me what I wanted."

"I remember."

"I want control," she said, opening her eyes. "Not like a king or anything. I just want to be able to control it, a little. My life. I don't want to get shoved around, by people or by fate or whatever. I just . . . I want it to be me who chooses."

"I know little of the way your world works, mistress," he said, coiling up onto the wall, then making a face that hung out beside her. "But that seems like a reasonable desire."

"Listen to these kids talk. Do you hear them?"

"They're scared of the storm."

"And of the sudden call to hide. And of being alone. So uncertain . . ."

In the other room she could hear the Stump, talking softly to one of her older helpers. "I don't know. It's not the day for a highstorm. I'll put the spheres out up top, just in case. I wish someone would tell us what was happening."

"I don't understand, mistress," Wyndle said. "What is it I'm supposed to get from this observation?"

"Hush, Voidbringer," she said, still listening. Hearing. Then, she paused and opened her eyes. She frowned and stood, crossing the room.

A boy with a scar on his face was talking to one of the other boys. He looked up at Lift. "Hey," he said. "I know you. You saw my mom, right? Did she say when she was coming back?"

What was his name again? "Mik?"

"Yeah," he said. "Look, I don't belong here, right?

I don't remember the last few weeks very well, but . . . I mean, I'm not an orphan. I've still got a mom."

It was him, the boy who had been dropped off the night before. *You were drooling then,* Lift thought. *And even at lunch, you were talking like an idiot. Storms. What did I do to you?* She couldn't heal people that were different in the head, or so she'd thought. What was the difference with him? Was it because he had a head wound, and wasn't born this way?

She didn't remember healing him. Storms . . . she said she wanted control, but she didn't even know how to use what she had. Her race to this place proved it.

The Stump strode back in with a large plate and began handing out pancakes to the children. She got to Lift, then handed her two. "This is the last," she said, wagging her finger.

"Thanks," Lift mumbled as the Stump moved on. The pancakes were cold, and unfortunately of a variety she'd already tried—the ones with sweet stuff in the middle. Her favorite. Maybe the Stump wasn't all bad.

She's a thief and a thug, Lift reminded herself as she ate, restoring her awesomeness. *She's laundering spheres and using an orphanage as cover.* But maybe even a thief and a thug could do some good along the way.

"I'm so confused," Wyndle said. "Mistress, what are you thinking?"

She looked toward the thick door to the outside.

The old man was surely dead by now. Nobody would care; likely nobody would notice. One old man, found dead in an alley after the storm.

But Lift . . . Lift would remember him.

"Come on," she said. She stepped over to the door. When the Stump's back was turned to scold a child, Lift pushed up the bar and slipped outside.

18

The hungry sky rumbled above, dark and angry. Lift knew that feeling. Too much time between meals, and looking to eat whatever it could find, never mind the cost.

The storm hadn't fully arrived yet, but from the distant lightning, it seemed that this new storm didn't have a stormwall. Its onset wouldn't be a sudden, majestic event, but instead a creeping advance. It loomed like a thug in an alley, knife out, waiting for prey to wander past.

Lift stepped up to the mouth of the alleyway beside the orphanage, then crept in, passing between shanties that looked far too flimsy to survive highstorms. Even if the city had been built to absolutely minimize winds, there was just so much *junk* in here. A particularly vigorous sneeze could leave half the people in the alley homeless.

They realized it too, as almost everyone here had gone to the storm bunkers. She did catch the odd face peeking suspiciously between rags draped on windows, anticipationspren growing up from the floor beside them like red streamers. They were people too stubborn, or perhaps too crazy, to be bothered. She didn't completely blame them. The government giving sudden, random orders and expecting everyone to hop? That was the sort of thing she usually ignored.

Except they should have seen the sky, heard the thunder. A flash of red lightning lit her surroundings. Today, these people should have listened.

She inched farther into the alleyway, entering a place of undefined shadows. With the clouds overhead—and everyone having taken their spheres away—the place was nearly impenetrable. So silent, the only sound that of the sky. Storms, was the old man actually in here? Maybe he was safe in a bunker somewhere. That scream from earlier could have been something unrelated, right?

No, she thought. *No, it wasn't.* She felt another chill run through her. Well, even if the old man was here, how would she find his body?

"Mistress," Wyndle whispered. "Oh, I don't like this place, mistress. Something's wrong."

Everything was wrong; it had been since Darkness had first stalked her. Lift continued on, past shadows that were probably laundry draped along strings between shanties. They looked like twisted, broken bodies in the gloom. Another flash of lightning from the approaching storm didn't help; the red light it cast made the walls and shanties seem painted with blood.

How long *was* this alleyway? She was relieved when, at last, she stumbled over something on the ground. She reached down, feeling at a clothed arm. A body.

I will remember you, Lift thought, leaning over and squinting, trying to make out the old man's shape.

"Mistress..." Wyndle whimpered. She felt him wrap around her leg and tighten there, like a child clinging to his mother.

What was that? She listened as the silence of the alley gave way to a clicking, scraping sound. It encircled her. And for the first time she noticed that the figure she was poking at didn't seem to be wrapped in a shiqua. The cloth on the arm was too stiff, too thick.

Mother, Lift thought, terrified. *What is happening?*

Lightning flashed, granting her a glimpse of the corpse. A woman's face stared upward with sightless eyes. A black and white uniform, painted crimson by the lightning and covered in some kind of silky substance.

Lift gasped and jumped backward, bumping into something behind her—another body. She spun, and the skittering, clicking sounds grew agitated. The next flash of lightning was bright enough for her to make out a body pressed against the wall of the alleyway, tied to part of a shanty, the head rolling to the side. She knew him, just as she knew the woman on the ground.

Darkness's two minions, Lift thought. *They're dead.*

"I heard an interesting idea once, while traveling in a land you will never visit."

Lift froze. It was the old man's voice.

"There are a group of people who believe that each day, when they sleep, they die," the old man continued. "They believe that consciousness doesn't continue— that if it is interrupted, a new soul is born when the body awakes."

Storms, storms, STORMS, Lift thought, spinning around. The walls seemed to be moving, shifting, sliding like they were covered in oil. She tried shying away from the corpses, but . . . she'd lost where they were. Was that the direction she'd come from, or did that lead deeper into this nightmare of an alleyway?

"This philosophy," the old man's voice said, "certainly has its problems, at least to an outside observer. What of memory, and continuity of culture, family, society? Well, the Omnithi teach that each are things you inherit in the morning from the previous soul that inhabited your body. Certain brain structures imprint memories, to help you live your single day of life as best you can."

"What are you?" Lift whispered, looking around frantically, trying to make sense of the darkness.

"What I find most interesting about these people is how they continue to exist at all," he said. "One would assume chaos would follow if each human sincerely believed that they had only one day to live. I wonder often what it says about you that these people with such dramatic beliefs live lives that are—basically— the same as the rest of you."

There, Lift thought, picking him out in the shadows. The shape of a man, though as lightning lit him she could see that he wasn't all there. Chunks were missing from his flesh. His right shoulder ended in a stump, and storms, he was naked, with strange holes in his stomach and thighs. Even one of his eyes was missing. There was no blood though, and in a quick succession of flashes she picked up something climbing his legs. Cremlings.

That was the skittering sound. Thousands upon thousands of cremlings coated the walls, each the size of a finger. Little beasts of chitin and legs clicking away and making that awful buzz.

"The thing about this philosophy is how difficult it is to disprove," the old man said. "How do you know that *you* are the same *you* as yesterday? You would never know if a new soul came to inhabit your body, so long as it had the same memories. But then . . . if it acts the same, and thinks it is you, why would it matter? What is it to be *you,* little Radiant?"

In the flashes of lightning—they were growing more common—she watched one of the cremlings crawl across his face, a bulbous protrusion hanging off its back. The thing crawled *into* the eye hole, and she realized that bulbous part was an eye. Other cremlings swarmed up and began filling in holes, forming the missing arm. Each had a portion on the back that resembled skin. It presented this outward, using its legs to interlock with the many others holding together on the inside of the body.

"To me," he said, "this is all no more than idle theory, as unlike you I do not sleep. At least, not all of me at once."

"What *are* you?" Lift said.

"Just another refugee."

Lift backed away. She didn't care anymore about going back in the direction she had come—so long as she got away from this thing.

"You needn't fear me," the old man said. "Your war is my war, and has been for millennia. Ancient Radiants named me friend and ally before everything went wrong. What wonderful days those were, before the Last Desolation. Days of . . . honor. Now gone, long gone."

"You killed these two people!" Lift hissed.

"In defense of myself." He chuckled. "I suppose that is a lie. They were not capable of killing me, so I can't plead self-defense, any more than a soldier could plead it in murdering a child. But they did ask, in not so many words, for a contest—and I gave it to them."

He stepped toward her, and a flash of lightning revealed him flexing his fingers on his newly formed hand as the thumb—a single cremling, with little spindly legs on the bottom—settled into place, tying itself into the others.

"But you," the thing said, "did not come for a contest, did you? We watch the others. The assassin. The surgeon. The liar. The highprince. But not you. The others all ignore you . . . and that, I hazard to predict, is a mistake."

He took out a sphere, bathing the place in a phantom glow, and smiled at her. She could see the lines crisscrossing his skin where the cremlings had fit themselves together, but they were nearly lost in the wrinkles of an aged body.

This was just the *likeness* of an old man though. A fabrication. Beneath that skin was not blood or muscle. It was hundreds of cremlings, pulling together to form a counterfeit man.

Many, many more of them still scuttled on the walls, now lit by his sphere. Lift could see that she'd somehow made it around the body of the fallen soldier, and was backing into a dead end between two shanties. She looked up. Didn't seem too difficult to climb, now that she had some light.

"If you flee," the thing noted, "he'll kill the one you wanted to save."

"You are just fine, I'm sure."

The monster chuckled. "Those two fools got it wrong. I'm not the one that Nale is chasing; he knows to stay away from me and my kind. No, there's someone else. He stalks them tonight, and *will* complete his task. Nale, madman, Herald of Justice, is not one to leave business unfinished."

Lift hesitated, hands in place on a shanty's eaves, ready to haul herself up and start climbing. The cremlings on the walls—she'd never seen so many at once—scuttled aside, making room for her to pass.

He knew to let her run, if she wanted to. Clever monster.

Nearby, bathed in cool light that seemed bright as a bonfire compared to what she'd stumbled through before, the creature unwrapped a black shiqua. He started winding it around his right arm.

"I like this place," he explained. "Where else would I have the excuse to cover my entire body? I've spent thousands of years breeding my hordelings, and still I can't make them fit together quite *right*. I can pass for human almost as well as a Siah can these days, I'd hazard, but anyone who looks closely finds something off. It's rather frustrating."

"What do you know about Darkness and his plans?" Lift demanded. "And Radiants, and Voidbringers, and *everything*?"

"That's quite the exhaustive list," he said. "And I confess, I am the wrong one to ask. My siblings are more interested in you Radiants. If you ever encounter another of the Sleepless, tell them you've spoken with Arclo. I'm certain it will gain you sympathy."

"That wasn't an answer. Not the kind I wanted."

"I'm not here to answer you, human. I'm here because I'm interested, and you are the source of my curiosity. When one achieves immortality, one must find purpose beyond the struggle to live, as old Axies always said."

"You seem to have found purpose in talkin' a whole bunch," Lift said. "Without being helpful to nobody." She scrambled up on top of the shanty, but didn't go any higher. Wyndle climbed the wall beside her, and the cremlings shied away from him. They could sense him?

"I'm helping with far more than your little personal

problem. I'm building a philosophy, one meaningful enough to span ages. You see, child, I can *grow* what I need. Is my mind becoming full? I can breed new hordelings specialized in holding memories. Do I need to sense what is going on in the city? Hordelings with extra eyes, or antennae to taste and hear, can solve that. Given time, I can make for my body nearly anything I need.

"But you . . . you are stuck with only one body. So how do you make it work? I have come to suspect that men in a city are each part of some greater organism they can't see—like the hordelings that make up my kind."

"That's great," Lift said. "But earlier, you said that Darkness was hunting someone *else*? You think he still hasn't killed his prey in the city?"

"Oh, I'm certain he hasn't. He hunts them right now. He will know that his minions have failed."

The storm rumbled above, close. She itched to leave, to find shelter. But . . .

"Tell me," she said. "Who is it?"

The creature smiled. "A secret. And we are in Tashikk, are we not? Shall we trade? You answer me honestly regarding my questions, and I'll give you a hint."

"Why me?" Lift said. "Why not bother someone else with these questions? At another time?"

"Oh, but you're so *interesting*." He wrapped the shiqua around his waist, then down his leg, then back up it, crossing to the other leg. His cremlings coursed around him. Several climbed up his face, and his eyes crawled out, new ones replacing them so that he went from being darkeyed to light.

He spoke as he dressed. "You, Lift, are different from anyone else. If each city is a creature, then you are a most special organ. Traveling from place to place, bringing change, transformation. You Knights Radiant . . . I must know how you see yourselves. It will be an important corner of my philosophy."

I am special, she thought. *I'm awesome.*

So why don't I know what to do?

The secret fear crept out. The creature kept talking his strange speech: about cities, people, and their places. He praised her, but each offhand comment about how special she was made her wince. A storm was almost here, and Darkness was about to murder in the night. All she could do was crouch in the presence of two corpses and a monster made of little squirming pieces.

Listen, Lift. Are you listening? People, they don't listen anymore.

"Yes, but how did the city of your birth know to create you?" the creature was saying. "I can breed individual pieces to do as I wish. What bred you? And why was this city able to summon you here now?"

Again that question. *Why are you here?*

"What if I'm *not* special," Lift whispered. "Would that be okay too?"

The creature stopped and looked at her. On the wall, Wyndle whimpered.

"What if I've been lying all along," Lift said. "What if I'm not *strictly* awesome. What if I don't know what to do?"

"Instinct will guide you, I'm sure."

I feel lost, like a soldier on a battlefield who can't remember which banner is hers, the guard captain's voice said.

Listening. She was listening, wasn't she?

Half the time, I get the sense that even kings are confused by the world. Ghenna the scribe's voice.

Nobody listened anymore.

I wish someone would tell us what was happening. The Stump's voice.

"What if you're wrong though?" Lift whispered. "What if 'instinct' doesn't guide us? What if everybody is frightened, and nobody has the answers?"

It was the conclusion that had always been too intimidating to consider. It terrified her.

Did it have to, though? She looked up at the wall,

at Wyndle surrounded by cremlings that snapped at him. Her own little Voidbringer.

Listen.

Lift hesitated, then patted him. She just . . . she just had to accept it, didn't she?

In a moment, she felt relief akin to her terror. She was in darkness, but well, maybe she'd manage anyway.

Lift stood up. "I left Azir because I was afraid. I came to Tashikk because that's where my starvin' feet took me. But tonight . . . tonight I *decided* to be here."

"What is this nonsense?" Arclo asked. "How does it help my philosophy?"

She cocked her head as a realization struck her, like a jolt of power. *Huh. Fancy that, would you?*

"I . . . didn't heal that boy," she whispered.

"What?"

"The Stump trades spheres for ones of lesser value, probably swapping dun ones for infused ones. She launders money because she *needs the Stormlight;* she probably feeds on it without realizing what she's doing!" Lift looked down at Arclo, grinning. "Don't you see? She takes care of the kids who were born sick, lets them stay. It's because her powers don't know how to heal those. The rest, though, they get better. They do it so suspiciously often that she's started to believe that kids must *come to her faking* to get food. The Stump . . . is a Radiant."

The Sleepless creature met her eyes, then sighed. "We will speak again another time. Like Nale, I am not one to leave tasks unfinished."

He tossed his sphere along the alleyway, and it plinked against stone, rolling back toward the orphanage. Lighting the way for Lift as she jumped down and started running.

19

The thunder chased her. Wind howled through the city's slots, windspren zipping past her, as if fleeing the advent of the strange storm. The wind pushed against Lift's back, blowing scraps of paper and refuse around her. She reached the small amphitheater at the mouth of the alley, and hazarded a glance behind her.

She stumbled to a stop, stunned.

The storm *surged* across the sky, a majestic and terrible black thunderhead coursing with red lightning. It was enormous, dominating the entire sky, wicked with flashes of inner light.

Raindrops started to pelt her, and though there was no stormwall, the wind was already growing tempestuous.

Wyndle grew in a circle around her. "Mistress? Mistress, oh, this is bad."

She stepped back, transfixed by the boiling mass of black and red. Lightning sprayed down across the slots, and thunder hit her with so much force, it felt as if she should have been flung backward.

"Mistress!"

"Inside," Lift said, scrambling toward the door into the orphanage. It was so dark, she could barely make out the wall. But as she arrived, she immediately noticed something wrong. The door was open.

Surely they'd closed it after she'd left? She slipped in. The room beyond was black, impenetrable, but feeling at the door told her that the bar had been cut right through. Probably from the outside, and with a weapon that sliced wood cleanly. A Shardblade.

Trembling, Lift felt for the cut portion of the bar on the floor, then managed to fit it into place, holding the door closed. She turned in the room, listening. She could hear the whimpers of the children, choked sobs.

"Mistress," Wyndle whispered. "You can't fight him."

I know.

"There are Words that you must speak."

They won't help.

Tonight, the Words were the easy part.

It was hard not to adopt the fear of the children

around her. Lift found herself trembling, and stopped somewhere in the center of the room. She couldn't creep along, stumbling over other kids, if she wanted to stop Darkness.

Somewhere distant in the multistory orphanage, she heard thumping. Firm, booted feet on the wooden floors of the second story.

Lift drew in her awesomeness, and started to glow. Light rose from her arms like steam from a hot griddle. It wasn't terribly bright, but in that pure-black room it was enough to show her the children she had heard. They grew quiet, watching her with awe.

"Darkness!" Lift shouted. "The one they call Nin, or Nale! Nakku, the Judge! I'm here."

The thumping above stopped. Lift crossed the room, stepping into the next one and looking up a stairwell. "It's me!" she shouted up it. "The one you tried—and failed—to kill in Azir."

The door to the amphitheater rattled as wind shook it, like someone was outside trying to get in. The footfalls started again, and Darkness appeared at the top of the stairs, holding an amethyst sphere in one hand, a glittering Shardblade in the other. The violet light lit his face from below, outlining his chin and cheeks, but leaving his eyes dark. They seemed hollow, like the sockets of the creature Lift had met outside.

"I am surprised to see you accept judgment," Darkness said. "I had thought you would remain in pre-sumed safety."

"Yeah," Lift called. "You know, the day the Al-mighty was handin' out brains to folks? I went out for flatbread that day."

"You come here during a highstorm," Darkness said. "You are trapped in here with me, and I know of your crimes in this city."

"But I got back by the time the Almighty was givin' out looks," Lift called. "What kept you?"

The insult appeared to have no effect, though it was one of her favorites. Darkness seemed to flow like smoke as he started down the stairs, footsteps grow-ing softer, uniform rippling in an unseen wind. Storms, but he looked so *official* in that outfit with the long cuffs, the crisp jacket. Like the very incarnation of law.

Lift scrambled to the right, away from the children, deeper into the orphanage's ground floor. She smelled spices in this direction, and let her nose guide her into a dark kitchen.

"Up the wall," she ordered Wyndle, who grew along it beside the doorway. Lift snatched a tuber from the counter, then grabbed on to Wyndle and climbed. She quieted her awesomeness, becoming dark as she reached the place where wall met ceiling, clinging to Wyndle's thin vines.

Darkness entered below, looking right, then left. He didn't look up, so when he stepped forward, Lift dropped behind him.

Darkness immediately spun, whipping that Shardblade around with a single-handed grip. It sheared through the wall of the doorway and passed a finger's width in front of Lift as she threw herself backward.

She hit the floor and burst alight with awesomeness, Slicking her backside so she slid across the floor away from him, eventually colliding with the wall just below the steps. She untangled her limbs and started climbing the steps on all fours.

"You're an insult to the order you would claim," Darkness said, striding after her.

"Sure, probably," Lift called. "Storms, I'm an insult to my own *self* most days."

"Of course you are," Darkness said, reaching the bottom of the steps. "That sentence has no meaning."

She stuck her tongue out at him. A totally *rational* and *reasonable* way to fight a demigod. He didn't seem to mind, but then, he wouldn't. He had a lump of crusty earwax for a heart. So tragic.

The second floor of the orphanage was filled with smaller rooms, to her left. To her right, another flight of steps led farther upward. Lift dashed left, choking down the uncooked longroot, looking for the Stump.

Had Darkness gotten to her? Several rooms held bunks for the children. So the Stump didn't make them sleep in that one big room; they'd probably gathered there because of the storm.

"Mistress!" Wyndle said. "Do you have a plan!"

"I can make Stormlight," Lift said, puffing and drawing a little awesomeness as she checked the room across the hall.

"Yes. Baffling, but true."

"He can't. And spheres are rare, 'cuz nobody expected the storm that came in the middle of the Weeping. So . . ."

"Ah . . . Maybe we wear him down!"

"Can't fight him," Lift said. "Seems the best alternative. Might have to sneak down and get more food though." Where *was* the Stump? No sign of her hiding in these rooms, but also no sign of her murdered corpse.

Lift ducked back into the hallway. Darkness dominated the other end, near the steps. He walked slowly toward her, Shardblade held in a strange reverse grip, with the dangerous end pointing out behind him.

Lift quieted her awesomeness and stopped glowing. She needed to run him out, and maybe make him think she was running low, so he wouldn't conserve.

"I am sorry I must do this," Darkness said. "Once I would have welcomed you as a sister."

"No," Lift said. "You're not really sorry, are you? Can you even *feel* something like sorrow?"

He stopped in the hallway, sphere still gripped before him for light. He actually seemed to be considering her question.

Well, time to move then. She couldn't afford to get cornered, and sometimes that meant charging at the guy with a starvin' Shardblade. He set himself in a swordsman's stance as she dashed toward him, then stepped forward to swing.

Lift shoved herself to the side and Slicked herself, dodging his sword and sliding along the ground to his left. She got past him, but something about it felt too easy. Darkness watched her with careful, discerning eyes. He'd expected to miss her, she was sure of it.

He spun and advanced on her again, stepping quickly to prevent her from getting down the steps to the ground floor. This positioned her near the steps going upward. Darkness seemed to want her to go that direction, so she resisted, backing up along the hallway. Unfortunately, there was only one room on this end, the one above the kitchen. She kicked open the door, looking in. The Stump's bedroom, with a dresser and bedding on the floor. No sign of the Stump herself.

Darkness continued to advance. "You are right. It seems I have finally released myself from the last vestiges of guilt I once felt at doing my duty. Honor has suffused me, changed me. It has been a long time coming."

"Great. So you're like . . . some kind of emotionless spren now."

"Hey," Wyndle said. "That's insulting."

"No," Darkness said, unable to hear Wyndle. "I'm merely a man, perfected." He waved toward her with his sphere. "Men need light, child. Alone we are in darkness, our movements random, based on subjective, changeable minds. But light is pure, and does not change based on our daily whims. To feel guilt at following a code with precision is wasted emotion."

"And other emotion isn't, in your opinion?"

"There are many useful emotions."

"Which you totally feel, all the time."

"Of course I do. . . ." He trailed off, and again seemed to be considering what she'd said. He cocked his head.

Lift jumped forward, Slicking herself again. He was guarding the way down, but she needed to slip past him anyway and head back below. Grab some food, keep him moving up and down until he ran out of power. She anticipated him swinging the sword, and as he did, she shoved herself to the side, her entire body Slick except the palm of her hand, for steering.

Darkness dropped his sphere and moved with sudden, unexpected speed, bursting afire with Stormlight. He dropped his Shardblade, which puffed away, and seized a knife from his belt. As Lift passed, he slammed it down and caught her clothing.

Storms! A normal wound, her awesomeness would have healed. If he'd tried to grab her, she'd have been too Slick, and would have wriggled away. But his knife bit into the wood and caught her by the tail of her overshirt, jerking her to a stop. Slicked as she was, she just kind of bounced and slid back toward him.

He put his hand to the side, summoning his Blade again as Lift frantically scrambled to free herself. The knife had sunk in deeply, and he kept one hand on it. Storms, he was strong! Lift bit his arm, to no effect. She struggled to pull off the overshirt, Slicking herself but not it.

His Shardblade appeared, and he raised it. Lift floundered, half blinded by her shirt, which she had halfway up over her head, obscuring most of her view. But she could feel that Blade descending on her—

Something went *smack,* and Darkness grunted.

Lift peeked out and saw the Stump standing on the steps upward, holding a large length of wood. Darkness shook his head, trying to clear it, and the Stump hit him again.

"Leave my kids alone, you monster," she growled at him. Water dripped from her. She'd taken her spheres up to the top of the building, to charge them. Of course that was where she'd been. She'd mentioned it earlier.

She raised the length of wood above her head. Darkness sighed, then swiped with his Blade, cutting her weapon in half. He pulled his dagger from the ground, freeing Lift. *Yes!*

Then he kicked her, sending her sliding down the hallway on her own Slickness, completely out of control.

"No!" Lift said, withdrawing her Slickness and rolling to a stop. Her vision shook as she saw Darkness turn on the Stump and grab her by the throat, then pull her off the steps and throw her to the ground. The old lady *cracked* as she hit, and fell limp, motionless.

He stabbed her then—not with his Blade, but with his *knife*. Why? Why not finish her?

He turned toward Lift, shadowed by the sphere he'd dropped, more a monster in that moment than the Sleepless thing Lift had seen in the alleyway.

"Still alive," he said to Lift. "But bleeding and unconscious." He kicked his sphere away. "She is too new to know how to feed on Stormlight in this state. You I'll have to impale and wait until you are truly dead. This one though, she can just bleed out. It's happening already."

I can heal her, Lift thought, desperate.

He knew that. He was baiting her.

She no longer had time to run him out of Storm-light. Pointing the Shardblade toward Lift, he was now truly just a silhouette. Darkness. True Darkness.

"I don't know what to do," Lift said.

"Say the Words," Wyndle said from beside her.

"I've said them, in my heart." But what good would they do?

Too few people listened to anything other than their own thoughts. But what good would listening do her here? All she could hear was the sound of the storm outside, lightning making the stones vibrate.

Thunder.

A new storm.

I can't defeat him. I've got to change him.

Listen.

Lift scrambled toward Darkness, summoning all of her remaining awesomeness. Darkness stepped forward, knife in one hand, Shardblade in the other. She got near to him, and again he guarded the steps downward. He obviously expected her either to go that way, or to stop at the Stump's unconscious body and try to heal her.

Lift did neither. She slid past them both, then turned and scrambled up the steps the Stump had come down a short time earlier.

Darkness cursed, swinging for her, but missing. She reached the third floor, and he charged after her.

"You're leaving her to die," he warned, giving chase as Lift found a smaller set of steps that led upward. Onto the roof, hopefully. Had to get him to follow . . .

A trapdoor in the ceiling barred her way, but she flung it open. She emerged into Damnation itself.

Terrible winds, broken by that awful red lightning. A horrific tempest of stinging rain. The "rooftop" was just the flat plain above the city, and Lift didn't spot the Stump's sphere cage. The rain was too blinding, the winds too terrible. She stepped from the trapdoor, but had to immediately huddle down, clinging to the rocks. Wyndle formed handholds for her, whimpering, holding her tightly.

Darkness emerged into the storm, rising from the hole in the clifftop. He saw her, then stepped forward, hefting his Shardblade like an axe.

He swung.

Lift screamed. She let go of Wyndle's vines and raised both hands above herself.

Wyndle sighed a long, soft sigh, melting away, transforming into a silvery length of metal.

She met Darkness's descending Blade with her own weapon. Not a sword. Lift didn't know crem about swords. Her weapon was just a silvery rod. It glowed in the darkness, and it blocked Darkness's blow, though his attack left her arms quivering.

Ow, Wyndle's voice said in her head.

Rain beat around them, and crimson lightning blasted down behind Darkness, leaving stark afterimages in Lift's eyes.

"You think you can fight me, child?" he growled, holding his Blade against her rod. "I who have lived immortal lives? I who have slain demigods and survived Desolations? I am the Herald of Justice."

"I will listen," Lift shouted, "to those who have been ignored!"

"What?" Darkness demanded.

"I heard what you said, Darkness! You were trying to prevent the Desolation. Look behind you! Deny what you're seeing!"

Lightning broke the air and howls rose in the city. Across the farmlands, the ruby glare revealed a huddled clump of people. A sorry, sad group. The poor parshmen who had been evicted.

The red lightning seemed to linger with them.

Their eyes were glowing.

"No," Nale said. The storm appeared to withdraw, briefly, around his words. "An . . . isolated event. Parshmen who had . . . who had survived with their forms . . ."

"You've failed," Lift shouted. "It's come."

Nale looked up at the thunderheads, rumbling with power, red light ceaselessly roiling within.

In that moment it seemed, strangely, that something within him emerged. It was stupid of her to think that with everything happening—the rain, the winds, the red lightning—she could see a difference in his eyes. But she swore that she could.

He seemed to focus, like a person waking up from a daze. His sword dropped from his fingers and puffed away into mist.

Then he slumped to his knees. "Storms. Jezrien . . . Ishar . . . It is true. I've failed." He bowed his head.

And he started weeping.

Puffing, feeling clammy and pained by the rain, Lift lowered her rod.

"I failed weeks ago," Nale said. "I knew it then. Oh, God. God the Almighty. It has returned!"

"I'm sorry," Lift said.

He looked to her, face lit red by the continuous lightning, tears mixing with the rain.

"You actually are," he said, then felt at his face. "I wasn't always like this. I *am* getting worse, aren't I? It's true."

"I don't know," Lift said. And then, by instinct, she did something she would never have thought possible.

She hugged Darkness.

He clung to her, this monster, this callous thing that had once been a Herald. He clung to her and wept in the storm. Then, with a crash of thunder, he pushed away from her. He stumbled on the slick rock, blown by the winds, then started to glow.

He shot into the dark sky and vanished. Lift heaved herself to her feet, and rushed down to heal the Stump.

20

"So you don't hafta be a sword," Lift said. She sat on the Stump's dresser, 'cuz the woman didn't have a proper desk for her to claim.

"A sword is traditional," Wyndle said.

"But you don't *hafta* be one."

"Obviously not," he said, sounding offended. "I must be metal. There is . . . a connection between our power, when condensed, and metal. That said, I've heard stories of spren becoming bows. I don't know how they'd make the string. Perhaps the Radiant carried their own string?"

Lift nodded, but she was barely listening. Who cared about bows and swords and stuff? This opened all *kinds* of more interesting possibilities.

"I do wonder what I'd look like as a sword," Wyndle said.

"You went around all day yesterday *complainin'* about me hitting someone with you!"

"I don't want to be a sword that one *swings,* obviously. But there is something stately about a Shardblade, something to be displayed. I would make a fine one, I should think. Very regal."

A knock came at the door downstairs, and Lift perked up. Unfortunately, it didn't sound like the scribe. She heard the Stump talking to someone who had a soft voice. The door closed shortly thereafter, and the Stump climbed the steps and entered Lift's room, carrying a large plate of pancakes.

Lift's stomach growled, and she stood up on the dresser. "Now, those are *your* pancakes, right?"

The Stump, looking as wizened as ever, stopped in place. "What does it matter?"

"It matters a *ton,*" Lift said. "Those aren't for the kids. You was gonna eat those yourself, right?"

"A dozen pancakes."

"Yes."

"Sure," the Stump said, rolling her eyes. "We'll pretend I was going to eat them all myself." She dropped them onto the dresser beside Lift, who started stuffing her face.

The Stump folded her bony arms, glancing over her shoulder.

"Who was at the door?" Lift asked.

"A mother. Come to insist, ashamed, that she wanted her child back."

"No kidding?" Lift said around bites of pancake. "Mik's mom actually came *back* for him?"

"Obviously she knew her son had been faking his illness. It was part of a scam to . . ." The Stump trailed off.

Huh, Lift thought. The mom couldn't have known that Mik had been healed—it had only happened yesterday, and the city was a mess following the storm. Fortunately, it wasn't as bad here as it could have been. Storms blowing one way or the other, in Yeddaw it didn't matter.

She was starvin' for information about the rest of the empire though. Seemed everything had gone wrong again, just in a new way this time.

Still, it was nice to hear a little good news. *Mik's mom actually came back. Guess it does happen once in a while.*

"I've been healing the children," the Stump said. She fingered her shiqua, which had been stabbed clean through by Darkness. Though she'd washed it, her blood had stained the cloth. "You're sure about this?"

"Yeah," Lift said around a bite of pancakes. "You should have a weird little thing hanging around you. Not me. Something *weirder.* Like a vine?"

"A spren," the Stump said. "Not like a vine. Like light reflected on a wall from a mirror . . ."

Lift glanced at Wyndle, who clung to the wall nearby. He nodded his vine face.

"Sure, that'll do. Congrats. You're a starvin' Knight Radiant, Stump. You've been feasting on spheres and healing kids. Probably makes up some for treatin' them like old laundry, eh?"

The Stump regarded Lift, who continued to munch on pancakes.

"I would have thought," the Stump said, "that Knights Radiant would be more majestic."

Lift scrunched up her face at the woman, then thrust her hand to the side and summoned Wyndle in the shape of a large, shimmering, silvery fork. A Shardfork, if you would.

She stabbed him into the pancakes, and unfortunately he went all the way through them, through the plate, and poked holes in the Stump's dresser. Still, she managed to pry up a pancake.

Lift took a big bite out of it. "Majestic as Damnation's own gonads," she proclaimed, then wagged Wyndle at the Stump. "That's saying it fancy-style, so my fork don't complain that I'm bein' crass."

The Stump seemed to have trouble coming up with a response to that, other than to stare at Lift with her jaw slack. She was rescued from looking dumb by someone pounding on the door below. One of the Stump's assistants opened it, but the woman herself hastened down the steps as soon as she heard who it was.

Lift dismissed Wyndle. Eating with your hands was way easier than eating with a fork, even a *very nice* fork. He formed back into a vine and curled up on the wall.

A short time later, Ghenna—the fat scribe from the Grand Indifference—stepped in. Judging by the way the Stump practically scraped the ground bowing to the woman, Lift judged that maybe Ghenna was more important than she'd assumed. Bet she didn't have a magic fork though.

"Normally," the scribe said, "I don't frequent such . . . domiciles as this. People usually come to me."

"I can tell," Lift said. "You obviously don't walk about very much."

The scribe sniffed at that, laying a satchel down on the bed. "His Imperial Majesty has been somewhat cross with us for cutting off the communication before. But he is understanding, as he must be, considering recent events."

"How's the empire doing?" Lift said, chewing on a pancake.

"Surviving," the scribe said. "But in chaos. Smaller villages were hit the worst, but although the storm was longer than a highstorm, its winds were not as bad. The worst was the lightning, which struck many who were unlucky enough to be out traveling."

She unpacked her tools: a spanreed board, paper, and pen. "His Imperial Majesty was very pleased that you contacted me, and he has already sent a message asking for the details of your health."

"Tell him I ain't eaten nearly enough pancakes," Lift said. "And I got this strange wart on my toe that keeps growin' back when I cut it off—I think because I heal myself with my awesomeness, which is starvin' inconvenient."

The scribe looked to her, then sighed and read the message that Gawx had sent her. The empire would survive, it said, but would take long to recover—particularly if the storm kept returning. And then there was the issue with the parshmen, which could prove an even greater danger. He didn't want to share state secrets over spanreed. Mostly he wanted to know if she was all right.

She kind of was. The scribe took to writing what Lift had told her, which would be enough to tell Gawx that she was well.

"Also," Lift added as the woman wrote, "I found another Radiant, only she's *real* old, and kinda looks like an underfed crab without no shell." She looked to the

Stump, and shrugged in a half apology. Surely she knew. She had mirrors, right?

"But she's actually kind of nice, and takes care of kids, so we should recruit her or something. If we fight Voidbringers, she can stare at them in a real mean way. They'll break down and tell her all about that time when they ate all the cookies and blamed it on Huisi, the girl what can't talk right."

Huisi snored anyway. She deserved it.

The scribe rolled her eyes, but wrote it. Lift nodded, finishing off the last pancake, a type with a real thick, almost mealy texture. "Okay," she proclaimed, standing up. "That's nine. What's the last one? I'm ready."

"The last one?" the Stump asked.

"Ten types of pancakes," Lift said. "It's why I came to this starvin' city. I've had nine now. Where's the last one?"

"The tenth is dedicated to Tashi," the scribe said absently as she wrote. "It is more a thought than a real entity. We bake nine, and leave the last in memory of Him."

"Wait," Lift said. "So there's only *nine*?"

"Yes."

"You all *lied* to me?"

"Not in so much—"

"Damnation! Wyndle, where'd that Skybreaker go? He's got to hear about this." She pointed at the scribe, then at the Stump. "He let you go for that whole money-laundering thing on my insistence. But when he hears you been *lying* about *pancakes,* I might not be able to hold him back."

Both of them stared at her, as if they thought they were innocent. Lift shook her head, then hopped off the dresser. "Excuse me," she said. "I gotta find the Radiant refreshment room. That's a fancy way of saying—"

"Down the stairs," the Stump said. "On the left. Same place it was this morning."

Lift left them, skipping down the stairs. Then she winked at one of the orphans watching in the main room before slipping out the front door, Wyndle on the ground beside her. She took a deep breath of the wet air, still soggy from the Everstorm. Refuse, broken boards, fallen branches, and discarded cloths littered the ground, snarling up at the many steps that jutted into the street.

But the city *had* survived, and people were already at work cleaning up. They'd lived their entire lives in the shadow of highstorms. They had adapted, and would continue to adapt.

Lift smiled, and started off along the street.

"We're leaving, then?" Wyndle asked.

"Yup."

"Just like that. No farewells."

"Nope."

"This is how it's going to be, isn't it? We'll wander into a city, but before there's time to put down roots, we'll be off again?"

"Sure," Lift said. "Though this time, I thought we might wander back to Azimir and the palace."

Wyndle was so stunned he let her pass him by. Then he zipped up to join her, eager as an axehound puppy. "Really? Oh, mistress. *Really?*"

"I figure," she said, "that nobody knows what they're doin' in life, right? So Gawx and the dusty viziers, they need me." She tapped her head. "I got it figured out."

"You've got what figured out?"

"Nothing at all," Lift said, with the utmost confidence.

But I will listen to those who are ignored, she thought. *Even people like Darkness, whom I'd rather never have heard. Maybe that will help.*

They wound through the city, then up the ramp, passing the guard captain, who was on duty there dealing with the even *larger* numbers of refugees coming to the city because they'd lost homes to the storm. She saw Lift, and nearly jumped out of her own boots in surprise.

Lift smiled and dug a pancake out of her pocket. This woman had been visited by Darkness because of her. That sort of thing earned you a debt. So she tossed the woman the pancake—which was really more of a pan*ball* at this point—then used the Stormlight she'd gotten from the ones she'd eaten to start healing the wounds of the refugees.

The guard captain watched in silence, holding her pancake, as Lift moved along the line breathing out Stormlight on everyone like she was tryin' to prove her breath didn't stink none.

It was starvin' hard work. But that was what pancakes was for, makin' kids feel better. Once she was done, and out of Stormlight, she tiredly waved and strode onto the plain outside the city.

"That was very benevolent of you," Wyndle said.

Lift shrugged. It didn't seem like it had made much of a difference—just a few people, and all. But they *were* the type that were forgotten and ignored by most.

"A better knight than me might stay," Lift said. "Heal everyone."

"A big project. Perhaps too big."

"And too small, all the same," Lift said, shoving her hands in her pockets, and walked for a time. She couldn't rightly explain it, but she knew that something larger was coming. And she needed to get to Azir.

Wyndle cleared his throat. Lift braced herself to hear him complain about something, like the silliness of walking all the way here from Azimir, only to walk right back two days later.

"... I was a very *regal* fork, wouldn't you say?" he asked instead.

Lift glanced at him, then grinned and cocked her head. "Y'know, Wyndle. It's strange, but ... I'm starting to think you might not be a Voidbringer after all."

POSTSCRIPT

Lift is one of my favorite characters from the Storm-light Archive, despite the fact that she has had very little screen time so far. I'm grooming her for a larger role in the future of the series, but this leaves me with some challenges. By the time Lift becomes a main Stormlight character, she'll have already sworn several of the oaths—and it feels wrong not to show readers the context of her swearing those oaths.

In working on Stormlight Three, I also noticed a small continuity issue. By the time we see him again in that book, the Herald Nale will have accepted that his work of many centuries (watching and making sure the Radiants don't return) is no longer relevant. This is a major shift in who he is and in his goals as an individual—and it felt wrong to have him undergo this realization offscreen.

Edgedancer, then, was an opportunity to fix both of these problems—and to give Lift her own showcase.

Part of my love of writing Lift has to do with the

way I get to slip character growth and meaningful moments into otherwise odd or silly-sounding phrases. Such as the fact that in the novelette from *Words of Radiance* she says she's been ten for three years (as a joke) can be foreshadowing with a laugh, which then develops into the fact that she actually thinks her aging stopped at ten. (And has good reason to think that.)

This isn't the sort of thing you can do as a writer with most characters.

I also used this story as an opportunity to show off the Tashikki people, who (not having any major viewpoint characters) were likely not going to get any major development in the main series.

The original plan for this novella was for it to be 18,000 words. It ended up at around 40,000. Ah well. That just happens sometimes. (Particularly when you are me.)

BRANDON SANDERSON is the author of,
amongst others, the Mistborn books, the Reckoners
novels and the epic fantasy that hit the *Sunday Times*
Hardback Bestsellers list, The Stormlight Archive.
He is currently working on new books in
each of these series.

• • •

Chosen by Robert Jordan's family to complete
Jordan's epic Wheel of Time Sequence, Brandon
Sanderson has gone on to become an internationally
bestselling author in his own right.

• • •

He lives with his family in Utah. Find out more on his
website, www.brandonsanderson.com, or you can
follow @brandsanderson on Twitter.

THE WAY OF KINGS

Brandon Sanderson

The result of more than ten years of planning, writing, and worldbuilding, *The Way of Kings* is but the opening movement of the Stormlight Archive, a bold masterpiece in the making

Speak again the ancient oaths,

Life before death.

Strength before weakness.

Journey before destination.

and return to men the Shards they once bore.

The Knights Radiant must stand again.

Roshar is a world of stone and storms. Its terrifying and frequent tempests have shaped ecology and civilisation alike.

It has been centuries since the fall of the Knights Radiant, but their Shardblades and Shardplate remain: mystical arms and armour that transform men into near-invincible warriors. Men trade kingdoms for Shardblades. Wars were fought for them, and won by them.

And now one such war, fought across the Shattered Plains, is about to swallow up a soldier, a brightlord and young woman scholar.

• • •

'Epic in every sense. Sanderson has built a world that leaps to life, a cast of varied characters and a vast history that slowly unfolds' *Guardian*

ABOUT GOLLANCZ

Gollancz is the oldest SF publishing imprint in the world. Since being founded in 1927 Gollancz has continued to publish a focused selection of bestselling and award-winning authors. The front-list includes **Ben Aaronovitch**, **Joe Abercrombie**, **Charlaine Harris**, **Joanne Harris**, **Joe Hill**, **Alastair Reynolds**, **Patrick Rothfuss**, **Nalini Singh** and **Brandon Sanderson**.

As one of the largest Science Fiction and Fantasy imprints in the UK it is no surprise we have one of the most extensive backlists in the world. Find high-quality SF on Gateway written by such authors as **Philip K. Dick**, **Ursula Le Guin**, **Connie Willis**, **Sir Arthur C. Clarke**, **Pat Cadigan**, **Michael Moorcock** and **George R.R. Martin**.

We also have a strand of publishing in translation, which includes French, Polish and Russian authors. Gollancz is home to more award-winning authors than any other imprint, with names including **Aliette de Bodard**, **M. John Harrison**, **Paul McAuley**, **Sarah Pinborough**, **Pierre Pevel**, **Justina Robson** and many more.

The SF Gateway
More than 3,000 classic, rare and previously out-of-print SF novels at your fingertips.
www.sfgateway.com

The Gollancz Blog
Bringing you news from our worlds to yours. Stories, interviews, articles and exclusive extracts just for you!
www.gollancz.co.uk

GOLLANCZ
LONDON